ONE WORD KILL

ALSO BY MARK LAWRENCE

The Broken Empire

Prince of Thorns
King of Thorns
Emperor of Thorns

Red Queen's War

Prince of Fools
The Liar's Key
The Wheel of Osheim

Book of the Ancestor

Red Sister
Grey Sister
Holy Sister

ONE WORD KILL

MARK LAWRENCE

47NORTH

Text copyright © 2019 by Mark Lawrence
All rights reserved.

Published by 47North, Seattle

www.apub.com

Amazon, the Amazon logo, and 47North are trademarks of Amazon.com, Inc., or its affiliates.

ISBN-13: 9781542042833 (hardcover)
ISBN-10: 1542042836 (hardcover)
ISBN-13: 9781503903265 (paperback)
ISBN-10: 1503903265 (paperback)

Cover design by Tom Sanderson

Printed in the United States of America

To everyone I've ever played D&D with.
May all your hits be critical.

CHAPTER 1

When Dr Parsons finally ran out of alternatives and reached the word 'cancer', he moved past it so quickly I almost thought I'd imagined it. He told me that boys of my age reacted very well to treatment. My mother took over the conversation at that point, launching them both into a lengthy discussion of survival rates. She always sought refuge in technical detail when life lurched into uncomfortable territory. To be honest, though, two minutes after being faced with a diagnosis of leukaemia is not the ideal time to have someone establish that when the medical profession says 'cured' it means 'survived five years'. Five years would break me into the 1990s at the grand old age of twenty.

That was the eighth day of January 1986. Dr Parsons, under pressure from my mother, revealed that around half of patients with my particular flavour of the disease would still be above ground five years after their diagnosis. 'Cured!' As unwilling to speculate as he was, I think even Dr Parsons would have assured me that the cancer would give me the next four weeks. But as it turned out, I would die even before February got into its stride.

Dr Ian Parsons was a tall, angular man with short black boring hair and absolutely no bedside manner. He looked deeply uncomfortable and, perhaps unfairly, I formed the impression that he felt it to be my fault that he found himself in the unfortunate position of having to tell a fifteen-year-old 'boy' he had at best a coin flip of reaching his twenties. I forgave him, though. I was both tall and angular myself and probably had no potential in me for a better bedside manner of my own. In general, I found other people to be a far greater mystery than, say, integral calculus, which my friends at school assured me was supposed to be difficult. I take pride in that 's'. Friends. I had two. Three, if you broadened the search beyond the school gates and counted Elton. Which I did. Four, if you counted the girl. Which, rather stupidly, I didn't.

I watched Dr Parsons and my mother talk. I had tuned out the actual words by that point and it was rather like watching the tennis with the sound off: a McEnroe-Lendl grudge match, questions and answers slammed across the scuffed table top. People look funny when you turn down the TV volume and they dance without music. When they talk without meaning it's the same thing. If you ignore the words, there's an honesty in the emotion that fleets across faces in conversation. Around my mother's eyes was a surprising desperation. If I had been listening to her I wouldn't have noticed it. She was always on top of any given situation, gathering the facts, completely in control of herself. Steely stare, serious grey hair – she'd gone grey in her twenties – narrow mouth carefully shaping each interrogation. But with the sound turned down she looked on the edge of tears. That worried me a lot. On Dr Parsons's pinched features a mixture of boredom and guilt. Perhaps the odd hint of surprise at my mother's depth of knowledge. A polymath. That's how people described her. My father used to say that she knew everything about everything. He died when I was twelve. He also had cancer, but an oncoming train cured him.

My father had been a mathematician. A famous one. At least as far as any mathematician or scientist not named Einstein can be famous. Other mathematicians in his field knew his name. Nobody else did.

On the day he died, he told me: 'The equations that govern the universe don't care about "now". You can ask them questions about this time or that time, but nowhere in the elegance of their mathematics is there any such thing as "now". The idea of one specific moment, one universal "now" racing along at sixty minutes an hour, slicing through the seconds, spitting the past out behind it and throwing itself into the future . . . that's just an artefact of consciousness, something entirely of our own making that the cosmos has no use for.'

We spoke like that.

'Nick?' My mother had obviously reached a conclusion and required me to say 'yes' before implementing the plan of action.

'I agree with the doctor,' I said.

'Well then.' Dr Parsons reached for the phone beside his notepad. 'I'll book you in for chemotherapy tomorrow. We've caught this early and with swift treatment the prognosis is . . .' He blanched somewhat beneath Mother's stare. 'Um. Better.'

I don't remember that first night spent at home, or rather all I have is the recollection of racing endlessly around a tight circle of thought: terror chasing its own tail, paralysis disguised as action.

The *Oxford English Dictionary* tells us that cancer is a noun and advises on pronunciation before declaring it a disease caused by an uncontrolled division of abnormal cells within the body. Put like that it doesn't sound too scary. Then it spoils the effect by noting the Greek root, *karkinos*, crab, said to have arisen from the swollen veins radiating from tumours that gave the impression of the many limbs of a crab.

At least they didn't name it after spiders. If I was going to be eaten alive, and I in no way wished to be, let it be by a crab rather than a spider.

Before my father's diagnosis, cancer had just been a word that occasionally poked itself from the background of general scariness into specifics. 'Mrs Ellard, she's got the cancer. It doesn't look good.' 'Simon's little brother? He won't be coming to school after all, dear.' 'The Big "C". Enough said.'

Afterwards it had become a monster that stalked behind me, and I walked on through my days steadfastly refusing to look its way in case it pounced. Turns out it didn't matter whether I looked or not. I got pounced on anyway.

I felt less scared at the hospital. Even though all statistics screamed that every white-tiled wall, every over-complicated bed, rubber tube, needle, and bag of clear fluids was an admission of failure. These people didn't know how to make me better, but they *acted* as if they did. They had crisp white uniforms, stethoscopes, a practised compassion. Their confidence partly filled the hole left when mine ran for the hills.

They call it chemo 'therapy' and sometimes the nurses would say things like, 'Time to take your medicine, Nick.' But nobody really thought of it as medicine. It's not. It's poison.

They used to poison you if you got syphilis. I have my mother to thank for this little nugget of information. There aren't many boys of fifteen who can say that. Not so long before my blood turned sour, but a sufficient number of decades to take you back before World War II and the use of penicillin, the only effective treatment for syphilis was to dose the victim with arsenic. The logic being that although arsenic is a deadly poison it is more deadly to the bacteria that cause the disease and, with careful judgement, the doctor can kill one of you without killing the other. Chemotherapy is much the same. The chemicals used may not be such well-known favourites of celebrated poisoners, but the idea remained unchanged. The aim was to make my blood into a soup toxic enough to kill the cancer cells while allowing the rest of me to struggle on.

I lay in a clean white bed beneath crisp cotton sheets on a ward where identical beds marched left and right partitioned by curtains that could be drawn for privacy. There were eleven of us in there, and three empty beds. About a third of us looked as if we'd just been pulled in off the street and stuck in a backless gown. Which to be fair is pretty much what had happened. Another third were losing their hair, some in alarming tufts, leaving an ugly patchwork of scalp, others suffering a general thinning like old men do. These kids looked unwell, black rings around their eyes as if they'd missed a couple of nights' sleep, pale-skinned, sweaty. Most of them were younger than me. A year older and they would have put me in Ealing General with the adults. The final third were bald and so thin you'd expect their bones to break through if they strained too hard. These kids behaved like old men and women, lying exhausted in their beds, eyes bright in dark hollows. When they looked at you it didn't take much imagination to see the skull beneath the skin.

They had us arranged by length in treatment so the ward looked rather like an assembly line, taking in healthy children at one end and spitting out corpses at the other.

An uncomfortably attractive nurse, who didn't look much older than me and called me *Nicky* in an annoyingly patronising voice, set up my line. The 'line' was a needle stuck into a vein in my arm, bound with about a mile of white gauze. The poison oozed through the needle, fed down a plastic tube from a clear bag on a stand beside the bed. It was a virulent yellow. I imagined radioactive urine might look much the same.

The parents and other visitors were shuffled out at half past five, some striding sharply toward the doors as if eager for fresh air, others dragging their heels, calling goodbyes. Some brave-faced, waiting to cry, some as grey and drawn as the child they were leaving behind. They went in a swirl of noise and empty promises, Mother with them. I didn't feel any more alone than I had done previously. It had only been a day, but I'd already discovered that cancer drops a bell jar over you, cutting you off from the world. You can still see it, but what it says is muffled and can't touch you. I hadn't called anyone. I hadn't told anyone. What would I say?

Nobody on the ward wanted to talk much, except for a girl called Eva in the bed opposite. She wanted to talk *too* much. The rest of us seemed to want to pretend this wasn't happening. To read our books and our comics, eat our sweets if we still had appetites, listen to the hospital radio on headphones that looked like white plastic tongs.

'They say some people don't vomit at all in the first week,' Eva told me.

I'd tried keeping my eyes glued to the pages of my book. I'd brought Bertrand Russell's *Principia Mathematica* because I wanted to see him build his marvellous mathematical house of cards. I needed to see the edifice raised in all its glory. Fresh, entire, complete, like a perfect son sprung whole from his father's brow. Then I would move on to read how a brilliant young mathematician named Kurt Gödel had brought Russell's great work crashing down eighteen years later. The genius's golden child shown to have feet of clay after all; tripped by Gödel's theorem of incompleteness and left in sprawling ruin. I guess Gödel's theorem was Russell's cancer, the uncontrolled division of abnormal cells deep within the mathematics, a taint that no amount of poison could drive from its veins.

Eva didn't care about any of that, any more than she cared about social signals like monosyllabic replies. Perhaps she had always been that way, or maybe she felt her diagnosis had given her licence.

'What're you reading? It looks dull. I don't like to read. I wish they had a telly in here.' Eva paused, for breath rather than for answers.

'Oh,' I said.

She said she was fourteen, but I would have believed her if she'd told me ten or twenty. She was thin and bland, with lank brown hair and a blade of a nose. Eva had tumours in her liver, she said. She asked me what that meant, but didn't listen when I told her. I'm not sure she even knew where her liver was or what it did.

'I bet I'm sick all night. This is my first night, you know. I'm going to be puking till we see yesterday's breakfast. Do you feel sick? I feel a bit ill already. Do you taste lemons?'

'No.' I wasn't sure what I felt like. Wound too tight. Ready to run. Hungry, sick, impatient, unable to stop the equations dancing and blurring on the page . . . a million things at once. But talking about it all wasn't one of those million things I felt like.

A nurse walked in through the double doors at our end of the ward, her stainless-steel trolley rattling along, laden with bags of virulent yellow toxin.

Behind her, down the long green corridor that led to the outside world, I saw my mother. She should have left the building ten minutes before. I expected her to be nearly halfway home by now, but there she was, facing a tall man in a dark coat. I couldn't tell much about him given the distance, but even so there was something suddenly familiar there. Not in that everyday sense of recognition but in the déjà vu way: an intense, almost fierce, certainty that I had seen this tableau before. The tall man in his dark coat, the fluorescent corridor lights gleaming on a perfectly bald head. He angled his face toward my mother in anger or concern while she, in a manner that made me doubt if she even were my mother, flinched away as if struck, retreating until her back pressed against the wall, her hands spread to either side like they were feeling for any exit on offer.

The doors swung closed, sealing off the view.

'I bet I'm sick all night. This is my first night, you know,' Eva said, and above us the lights dimmed and then for a second shone brighter than they should.

'Didn't you just tell me that?' I asked, glancing at the needle in my arm, the yellow poison queuing for entry.

A momentary frown and she carried on. 'I'm going to be puking till we see yesterday's breakfast. Do you feel sick? I feel a bit ill already. Do you taste lemons?'

CHAPTER 2

If crisp white linen and no-nonsense smiles could cure cancer nobody would ever die of it. Sadly, these were merely the window dressings of the National Health Service. I lay in their metal bed at the business end of a long needle and let their poison leak into my veins. Eva talked at me from across the ward, endlessly. I thought the bag dangling beside me would run out of its chemical soup before she ran out of her inane nonsense. But then she did run out, and shortly after began to retch into the cardboard bowl the nurse had brought her. And I realised that she was just scared; a scared little girl whose parents had left her alone with a fatal disease. And I knew I'd been a piece of shit. Again. And the sour smell of her vomit reached me, and I felt sick myself.

'It'll be OK, Eva.' I sounded awkward, even to myself. 'Hang in there.'

She didn't reply, just kept her head bowed over the bowl, a line of drool reaching down to join her to the contents.

I looked away, up toward the painful brightness of the ceiling. The chemo bag hung there like an evil yellow raindrop, like those big teardrop vases full of different coloured liquids that they used to put in chemists' windows. The yellow filled my vision, the ceiling lights focused through it.

'Nick!'

'Huh . . . What?'

'Roll, you dweeb.' Elton looked pointedly at the table in front of me.

I stood suddenly, toppling my chair and jolting the table. Half a dozen inch-high lead figures fell over, three of them armoured and carrying swords. The other three were larger and brown . . . ogres. Simon had painted those, brilliantly as always. His miniatures made ours look like toddlers had been jabbing at them with the sort of paintbrushes you use on walls.

'What the fuck is going on?' I felt twenty feet tall. Vertigo wanted to drag me down and send me crashing onto the table among all the dice and figures, sheets of paper, rulebooks, cans of coke.

'Nice work, moron!' John snorted and shook his head. Quite how John came to be in our Dungeons & Dragons group I'd never really figured out. Handsome, popular, at ease in his own skin. He wasn't the type. Wasn't *our* type. Which was probably why he kept our association secret at school. That hurt less that you'd think it would. I guess I was just pathetically grateful to be liked by someone 'normal'.

Simon was already setting the figures back up amid the sprawl of character sheets and maps, his hands remarkably delicate. Somehow, I always expected Simon's hands to be as fat and clumsy as the rest of him, but the boy could be a brain surgeon one day. He reconstructed the scene with perfect accuracy, muttering reminders to himself. Simon never forgot a thing. He knew pi to more decimal places than any sane person would want to. I sometimes joked that it was an irrational feat of memory. A maths joke. Nobody ever got it.

'Roll already!' Elton arched an eyebrow at me. I knew the expression. It was often followed by a demonstration of a karate move where Elton would talk you through the attack as he put you on your arse in slow motion. Even at quarter speed there wasn't much you could do about it. Elton knew his stuff. His oldest brother was a black belt and the other three were heading in that direction. All five of them lived in the tiny flat their parents had managed to secure after getting off the boat from Madagascar. Five was too many for the place. With their parents, there were seven of them.

Still confused, I reached for the twenty-sided die.

'D6!' Simon thrust a handful of six-sided dice at me. Focused, impatient. 'Damage roll.'

'Get with the programme, Nick.' John leaned his chair back on two legs, showing that easy grin of his. 'No daydreaming on the job!'

'But . . .' I looked around the room. Simon's bedroom, crowded with books and collectables. Fantasy and science fiction novels, and a shameful section on trains that Simon clung on to despite the fact that *even* Dungeons & Dragons nerds thought those were deeply uncool. 'But . . .' My hand tightened around the dice. I squeezed until the corners bit, trying to shake myself out of this dream. 'I've been here before. Done this before.'

'Yes . . .' said Elton. 'The last time you cast a fireball on a bunch of monsters. Roll the damn damage.'

'I mean . . . this is last week.'

'Hah!' John's one annoying habit was that he spoke his laughs. He didn't laugh like a normal person . . . he said 'hah'. It made me less willing to trust him. Laughter should be unguarded even if nothing else is. 'You're pulling a *Back to the Future* on us!'

'N-no.' Simon always stuttered when building up to a joke. 'H-he's the Terminator.'

'Sent from the future to kill us!' Elton grinned. He did the Schwarzenegger voice. 'Give me your clothes!' A wider grin as he brushed imaginary dust off his shoulder. 'Dream on, boy. You can't touch this. It's called style.'

'I was in an oncology ward . . .'

'Onk-what-ogy?' John snorted.

'Ward?' Simon frowned. 'Like a hospital?'

'Cancer.' A scowl from Elton. 'Not cool, dude. That shit's not funny.'

'I'll prove it! I'll . . .' The dice fell from my hand and I sat down. I grabbed a pen, and while the others leaned over to add up the numbers I'd rolled, I pushed aside the edge of the gaming mat and began to write, pressing hard enough to score the polished wood.

'That's you done, Nicky.'

'What?' I blinked. The pretty nurse, Lisa, was reaching for my arm. I snatched it away.

'Easy.' She smiled. 'You're done. The needle can come out now.' She started to unwind the gauze below my elbow. Above her head, the chemo bag, once pregnant with venom like the sacs behind a snake's fangs, hung flaccid, drained of all but a few yellow drops. 'Where did you wander off to then?'

'Sorry?'

'Away with the pixies, you were. Gazing up there somewhere.' She unwound the last turn and took hold of the needle, ready with a square of cotton wool for any bleeding.

'Last week. I was last week.' I stiffened as the needle came out. It stung rather than hurt, but the sensation was unpleasant. 'Does this stuff give you nightmares?'

Lisa pursed her lips and straightened up. 'A lot of children get bad dreams in hospital. Don't worry about it. We'll be checking on you through the night to make sure you're not having a bad reaction. You can press the call button if you feel sick. There are medicines we can give you.'

'Medicines for the medicine.' I blinked. Part of me hadn't quite left Simon's room yet. I could still feel the impression of the pen on my fingers. I looked down, expecting to find them inky, but they were clean. 'I mean, can you get hallucinations and stuff?'

Lisa shook her head. She had her hair tied up. 'Don't you worry about any of that, Nicky. You'll be fine.'

She walked away with the bundled gauze and needle on her tray. I watched her go.

A modest increase in the windowless ward's general brightness and clatter signalled the arrival of morning, along with a dawn chorus of greetings at the nurses' station as the night shift swapped with the day shift. I rolled over, bleary-eyed and tangled in my sheets. I felt sore, as if I really had spent the night running from myself down endless corridors, rather than just having had a rather unimaginative dream.

I'd slept badly. The pain in my joints, the agony that lanced without warning along the bones of my arms and legs, had kept lifting me from the shallow pit of my dreams. When the aching had first started, Mother had said they were growing pains and that most boys got them if they decided to gain a foot in height in a year. The growing pains kept growing, though. They were the symptoms that had taken me to the local doctor's office to be dismissed and then marched back again three weeks later behind my indignant mother. At that point they had humoured us with an appointment at the hospital for 'tests'.

After that first long chemo night my mother arrived promptly at nine, for visiting hours. The parents flowed in and she entered midstream. Where curiosity had other mothers and fathers rubbernecking all the way down the ward, Mother kept her gaze pinned to me, refusing to look at the other children.

'How are you feeling, dear?'

'I . . . I don't know.' I saw her face tense. 'Fine!' I said. Her eyebrows arched. 'Not too bad.' I settled for something close to the truth. 'Strange.'

'They said to expect nausea at some point.' Her eyes flickered to the sick bowl on my table. 'And the hair loss, of course.' She looked up at my fringe as if expecting to see it thinning. As if the unruly mop that had been riding about on my head for fifteen years might just have been waiting all this time for an excuse to leave and would slide off at the first opportunity.

'Who was that man you were talking to in the corridor last night?'

'What man?' She looked guilty at once. I'd never seen her look guilty before. Except maybe when she told me the train had killed my father instantly. I read in the local newspaper that he had been struck a glancing blow and died in hospital that night. That always bothered me. He'd chosen to end it quickly and failed, even with the help of a train. As if when the universe gave him his cancer it was determined that he suffer, one way or the other.

'The tall guy, bald.' I touched my hair. 'And why were you here so late?'

'I forgot something. Had to come back.' She waved down the nurse passing the end of my bed. 'Is Nicholas going to be allowed home today?'

'The doctors have been through, looked at the notes. Everything's fine.' A smile full of professional optimism. 'You can take Nicholas home whenever he feels ready. We'll be sending you confirmation of his next appointment, same time next week – another overnight stay, I'm afraid.'

'Well, that's excellent.' Mother echoed the woman's smile and turned to me. 'Ready to go?'

And that was that. Five minutes later I was walking out of there into the big wide world as if nothing had happened and my veins weren't full of toxin and I hadn't left behind half a dozen dying children who looked like those bodies in the concentration camp footage they showed us in history class. Eva had to stay. At least until she could keep fluids down, they said. I stopped at the end of her bed to say goodbye. She looked sick, but she was back to voicing every thought that ran through her head, even with her parents on either side.

'Uh. See you next week, I guess.' I felt I should do something. Maybe reach out and pat her foot where it tented the sheet close by. But I didn't. Not with her mother and father looking at me, accusation in their eyes. *Why aren't you sick, too?*

Eva managed a smile. 'I'll see you next week. I hadn't thought of that. We'll be seeing each other every time now. We're . . . what's the word? Syncrotised? This is my mum and dad. See you, Nick! See you!' She kept talking as I followed Mother out, as if the conversation were a rope and if she only kept it unbroken I would be held by it, unable to leave.

It's always a shock, when you've been hit by some calamity, to see the world go about its business with perfect indifference. When Elvis dies, when Charles marries Diana, you feel you're part of things, that everyone is moved by the same current, even if they really don't want to be. But turn that around and you discover that your father dying or your blood turning against you doesn't make the slightest impact. Not only does the world keep turning and the birds keep singing, but the buses run, people scurry to work bound about with their own cares, and the man in the corner shop still snarls at you as if taking your money is a great imposition.

We drove home through the Friday pre-lunch traffic. There's no good time to drive in London, just less-worse times. The others would be at school. Second day back. The others. As if I were still part of them, not a modern-day leper with a soon-to-be-shiny scalp and a drip stand in place of sores and a bell that tolls 'Unclean! Unclean!' It doesn't matter what the doctors say, there's no fatal disease that doesn't feel contagious to the person sitting next to you.

John and Simon went to the same school as me, Maylert, a private school nestled up against the banks of the Thames. You didn't have to be rich to go there, just not poor. Some were rich, though. John's grandfather had been a lord! His father did something in the city. Shovelling money into buckets by the look of the Richmond mansion they lived in. Simon's parents weren't rich, a teacher and a university lecturer, but they stumped up the fees so that Simon would get beaten less viciously and by a better class of bully. Simon had 'victim' written all over him: overweight, obsessive, and blessed with a set of social graces that made me look suave.

Elton went to some dangerous-sounding comprehensive not far from Simon's house. We all professed to envy him as, unlike Maylert, his was a mixed school and girls made up half of every class. While that was an education we were all sorely in need of, in truth only John stood a chance of securing a girlfriend, unless studiously ignoring a girl and awkward silences really were the key to the art of seduction.

'What do you want for lunch?' Mother's voice was a fraction too bright, a touch brittle. She never made me lunch. I heated up a tin of mushroom soup. Or forgot to heat one up and wondered later why I was hungry.

'Soup?' I wanted to say that I wanted my life back. Instead, I trekked upstairs to my bedroom and fell onto the bed that I'd grown up sleeping in. Once it had been a three-year-old Nicky who bounced onto his first 'big boy bed', now an over-tall fifteen-year-old, too skinny, all sharp elbows and greasy hair, folded onto the much-punished mattress and stared at the ceiling. I lay there trying to ignore the dull ache of my hips and wrists. Too many thoughts tried to crowd in at once, with the net effect that none of them managed to get a space.

The next thing I knew it was dark. I sat up disoriented and a blanket slid from me. My bed. Still my bed.

A sharp noise broke the darkness. A pebble against the window. I stumbled across the room and flicked the light switch. My room. As I left it. A bowl of cold soup the only addition. I flicked the light back off and went to the window. Two figures stood at the base of the nearest street-light in the pooled sodium glow. The taller one was John. He waved.

A minute later I was leaving the front door, zipping my parka as I went.

'That was quick! Sleep in your clothes?'

'Something like that.' I looked past him. The girl was still leaning against the lamppost, breath pluming before her. She had black hair, short-ish, a black coat, pale skin. 'What time is it?'

'Coming up to midnight maybe.' John shrugged. 'Thought we'd come check on you. Nicky Hayes doesn't miss school two days in a row unless he's dying.' He glanced back at the girl. 'He look dead to you, Mia?' He'd dialled his accent back to as close to common as it would go. Which wasn't very close, but a one-eighty from the upper-crust drawl he used at school.

Mia looked at me as if John's question weren't rhetorical. 'Some life left in him yet, probably.' She was Elton's friend. Our first and last encounter had been two weeks ago when he brought her unannounced to Simon's house for the D&D session. Simon and I had gone into shock, unable to utter more than grunts, as if we were on stage in a school drama lesson waiting for the mockery. It had been the worst session ever. What she was doing with John, I had no idea. I kept staring from her to him like an idiot, trying to imagine how he had got her number. And then, armed with that, how he had had the superhuman courage to call her.

'We're going down by the river.' John pulled a can of Fosters from his coat and pushed it at me. 'Come on, we'll puff some weed.' He mimed drawing on a joint.

I took the can, finding it warmer than expected. 'I guess.' My stomach growled, a hollow hunger gnawing at me. I thought of the cold mushroom soup and felt nauseous.

John led the way. If you say 'the river' in Richmond you mean the Thames, the broad grey-green expanse of water that slides its way through London. Unless you're John, in which case you mean Beverly Brook. It's a stream that hurries across Richmond Park. And if 'the river' is too big a name for the brook, then 'the park' is too small a name for Richmond Park, which, rather than being two football fields and some swings, is a proper seventh-century hunting reserve with accompanying deer, whittled down to a square mile of forest and field amid the tight-packed chaos of the city.

At the park's Wessex Road gates, a cruel hand reached in to twist my guts. Before I knew it, I was doubled up by the fence with one hand clutching the iron bars. I retched and retched again, acid burning my throat, spitting drool at the base of the gatepost.

'Shit, you *were* ill!' John backed away.

'I'll be OK.' I straightened up. I felt like crap, my mouth watering, hands trembling. Never let it be said that I don't know how to make a good impression with the ladies. 'Come on.'

We came to the dirty bank along a wooded path so dark I could barely see the trees. Without the pervasive London glow, even following the path would have been impossible. I hobbled along, wincing at the shooting pains in the long bones of my legs. It's amazing how much harder it is to dismiss a discomfort when someone changes the label on it from 'growing pains' to 'leukaemia'. Mia walked ahead beside John and they exchanged a mutter every so often. Sleep still had its last hooks in me, and their words floated under my hearing, incomprehensible.

'That's a brook?' Mia seemed unimpressed by the few black yards of water between us and the bushes on the other side.

'In America they'd call it a creek.' John had been to the States for his two previous summers. Perhaps he was unconscious of how quickly he referenced that fact in any conversation. He rummaged in his coat pocket again and brought out what looked like a cigarette with a middle-aged spread.

'You don't smoke,' I said.

'It's herb, man.' John sounded like what he was, a posh boy trying to impersonate a Rasta, and failing badly.

'I thought you were joking.' The words escaped me before I realised how many cool points I had just blown away in front of the only girl I knew. 'Did Elton . . . ?'

'Don't be stupid.' John snorted.

'Elton's dad would kill him if he touched this stuff.' Mia smiled. 'His mum, too. And his brothers. John bought it off me. I know a guy.' She shrugged.

'I . . . don't have a light.' John patted his chest as if a cigarette lighter or matches were the sort of thing he might reasonably expect to find in his inner pocket.

Mia sighed and produced a flame from a silver lighter, cupping it with her other hand.

The glowing tip of John's joint tracked toward his face. He put the cold end to his lips and puffed a great cloud of smoke. 'Great.' He creaked the word through his effort to suppress a cough and offered the joint to me. 'Try it.'

John's look of amazement when I actually took it was comical.

The voices of a dozen responsible adults rose along with the hand lifting it toward my mouth. Their protests rang in the back of my mind:

Mrs Green, a favourite teacher in my second year, shrill, denouncing; Mother, stern and disappointed; Mr Stanley from chess club, disapproving. I blocked them out. I had cancer. The biggest C. Why not live a little? Taste what was on offer before the fates swept it all beyond my reach.

I put my lips where John's had been and inhaled. I might not have smoked, but I knew how to do it. Smoke filled my lungs like cool fire. I held it there until a tickle sprang up and became a demand and I coughed it out.

'Easy, Nicky-boy!' John never talked like that. This was for Mia. He slapped my back hard enough to stagger me toward the water.

I caught a foot on a root and almost pitched into the brook but managed to regain my balance with nothing worse than muddy shoes. Coughing, I went back, something angry on my tongue . . . but the figure standing on the path stole away whatever I was going to say.

'There's someone back there,' I said, not taking my eyes from the black shape in the shadows.

John shrugged and passed the red ember of the joint to Mia. 'It's a free country.'

'You see him, though?' It didn't feel right: the man on our path, motionless, watching, made monstrous by the inky tree-haunted spaces around him.

John looked again. 'It's just some guy.' He sounded uneasy, though, bravado gone.

'We should go.' Mia pinched out the joint, serious. She knew something was wrong.

'Sure.' John led us off, eager now. Not back the way we came, but along the path that tracked the river. I followed, last, and the cold night seemed to echo around me. From the corner of my eye I saw phantoms, couples walking arm in arm, boys chasing each other, a woman with a dog, as if ghostly impressions of the park's visitors had returned to repeat their day's walks. None of them lasted if I turned to look at them, breaking apart like John's clouds of smoke. My head felt too heavy and the world kept rotating when I stopped moving. One drag on a joint and I was high already?

'He's coming!' Mia, her voice tight. I glanced back and saw the man advance, one black shape detaching from another, and the faintest gleam from a bald skull.

'Run!' John broke into a sprint.

It's a free country. The phrase whispered itself around me as I tried to run, too, brushing away the ghosts of a mother and child ambling down the path.

After that a panic took hold and we were all three fleeing with the focused urgency that is the gift of real fear and is stolen away when fear grows into terror. A swift nightmare of bushes, clawing branches, and blind corners followed.

'Jesus!' John leaned against the brick gatepost, hauling in his breath. 'What were we even running for?' He tried to laugh but started choking.

'I don't know.' I looked back into the blackness behind us. 'Got spooked, I guess. Probably some sad old flasher.'

'Well, that was fun.' Mia looked pale, any aura of coolness dispelled. 'Must do it again next year.'

'Hah.' John managed his laugh. 'We settled one thing.'

'What?' I asked.

'You can't be that sick, Hayes. You beat us both to the gate!'

And it was true; the pains that had seen me hobble to the river were gone, though whether it was the fear, the cannabis, or the strangeness of the night that had driven them away, I didn't know.

CHAPTER 3

'You're still going?'

'Yes, I told you.' I carried on buttoning my coat.

'You didn't have any breakfast.' Mother was wearing that tight, accusing look of hers.

'I'll get something at Simon's.' I snatched up my bag and reached for the door.

'Nicholas.' The full name. That always meant a lecture incoming.

'I'm fine.' A touch too harsh; I saw the hurt on her face. 'If I don't feel well, I'll come home.'

'I'll come and get you if you ring—'

I closed the door on her and hurried out into the day, a cold one, brittle with frost. The pain was back, shooting along my limbs, grinding in my hips. I bit down and kept to a brisk walk. *Aggressive.* That's how they described the worst cancer. Maybe I needed some aggression myself if I were going to win the fight.

It was a shock to find out how quickly I could be reduced to a shambling old man, moving cautiously around the set of aches and pains that now defined me. I wanted last month back. I wanted to marvel in the unappreciated joy of a pain-free body, to stride without a twinge or even the worry that there might be one. A month ago, I'd thought myself invincible. A few weeks on, a treacherous body I couldn't trust or command, and it felt as if my youth had run from me. Milk from a toppled bottle.

I walked the streets of Richmond wrapped in my own thoughts, puffing frosty breaths before me. Last night's smoke came to mind. The phantoms must have been the drug's work. Who knew what shit got into the resin Mia's 'guy' had supplied. The stalker? Well, he was just that. Or some old bloke out walking his dog. And why not? It was, after all, a free country.

I would be early to Simon's, but I'd woken early, too, and had been unable to lie in.

On the corner of Broad Street I saw Michael Devis, just leaning there, against the wall, fag in his hand. I went round by Foss Way to avoid him. Devis was my almost-bully, always testing, not quite sure enough of himself to do the job the way you saw it in the films, but enough to make me miserable. Sometimes I imagined what it would be like to just punch the bastard in the face, full out. But I didn't think I ever would. I'd tremble and stutter, and turn away like I always did, and it would be a toss-up whether I hated him or myself more. You would think that having cancer would override all those lesser fears; that I could stride up to Devis and poke him in the eye; that I could talk to Mia like she was a human being rather than some alien beamed down from the mothership. But life didn't seem to work like that. Which was a bummer, really.

Devis had started to get on my case about two years earlier. It had been when I'd taken up Dungeons & Dragons with Simon and a couple of others. Devis had smelled weakness. Difference. It hadn't been hard. I don't want to attribute some sort of superpower to the git. Playing games at our age might have been enough on its own. Boards and dice are the accessories of childhood: Monopoly at Christmas; Cluedo with your parents; popping the dice bubble to take your turn at Sorry. Bring that into school as a teenager and you're asking for trouble.

Lost in my thoughts, I almost walked right into Ian Rust. Maylert gets its pupils from all over London. I had to take the tube and change at Hammersmith. So, by rights, I could expect to walk down a street in Richmond without seeing any Maylert's boys. Seeing one was unusual. Turning off one road to avoid the biggest bully in your year, to then run into the school psychopath was the worst kind of luck. Well. Not cancer-bad, but cancer is quiet, hidden, slow. A monster in your face, on the other hand, is more immediately terrifying.

'What the hell are you doing?' Ian Rust was in the year two above mine. The fact he hadn't been expelled yet spoke volumes about his ability to manipulate both authority and victims.

'Sorry.' I hadn't bumped into him, but I'd been on course to. Now I tried to step around, but he blocked me, moving to the left, then the right, arms spread.

'Where you going?' A cruel smile. It was hard to imagine he had any other kind.

Ian Rust wasn't big. I was taller. He was scrawny. He didn't look a threat. Not until you looked him in the eye. They say he set an old homeless man on fire. That's probably a lie. I didn't see anything like that in the gazette. But you only had to spend a short time in his presence to believe that he would do something like that, just for fun. 'Where you off to?'

'Friend.' My mouth had gone too dry for words. I kept swallowing. I wanted to piss. I was every rabbit in every headlight, waiting to be road kill.

'*You* have friends?'

I don't think Rust knew my name even, but he knew me by sight, knew I went to the school and was therefore part of the herd he preyed on. People think you need to be big to be scary. They see boxers, big muscles, long arms, huge guys, and think that's what matters on the streets. What really matters in real life, though, is how far you're prepared to go and how quickly. Most disputes work to a strict choreography of display and threat. The escalation proceeds through a series of steps agreed by silent tradition. Everyone knows what they're getting into and both the exit and the stakes are clear.

What made Rust frightening was that he didn't seem to understand those rules. Being strong is all well and good, but if one of the rugby team got in Ian Rust's way, he would probably end up with a ballpoint pen in his eye before he'd even got to the shoving stage.

'I . . .' I could barely get a word out. Nausea bit deep, creating the real possibility I might vomit on him.

Rust simply watched me, delighted by my distress, and then, as if a light had been turned off, his smile vanished. He snatched the sports bag from my hand and unzipped it. A sneer. He tipped the contents onto the pavement: map and notes from the last game, my character sheet, dice, an apple that Mother had snuck in there last week, all bouncing on the paving slabs now, fluttering down into dirty puddles.

'Piss off.' He dropped the empty bag and carried on his way, kicking the apple ahead of him. Quite possibly he was off to meet with Devis on his corner in Broad Street. Devis was supposedly with Rust when he burned the tramp. A minion rather than a partner in crime.

I stood there, dismissed, full of fight-or-flight adrenaline, hating Rust and the way he'd made me feel. Angry, I knelt to gather my stuff. By the time I'd recovered all the pages and tried to wipe them down, he was long gone. I walked on, trying to shake away that mix of rage and terror, gripping my bag as if it might be Rust's throat.

Before reaching Simon's house I'd imagined half a dozen scenarios for how my encounter with Rust might have played out, all complex, visceral, and almost as scary as the real thing. And that's what united the four weirdos who were about to settle around Simon's gaming table and play out stories of magic and monsters. That's the common thread running through all the diverse hordes of nerds and geeks who turned up to the conventions and gatherings, who queued outside Games Workshop for the latest rulebook. We were all of us consumed by our own imagination, victims of it, haunted by impossibles, set alight by our own visions, and by other people's. We weren't the flamboyant artsy creatives, the darlings who would walk the boards beneath the hot eye of the spotlight, or dance, or paint, or even write novels. We were a tribe who had always felt as if we were locked into a box that we couldn't see. And when D&D came along, suddenly we saw both the box and the key.

'Got some new orcs to show you.'

Simon left the door half open and headed for the stairs. He never once said hello when he opened the door. You'd knock, and he'd pull it back like he'd been stood there staring at it for an hour. Even when you were early. Half the time he would just pitch in with the next line in the last conversation you'd had, as if a day or a week hadn't passed.

'Hello, Nick, how's it hanging?' Simon's mum called from the kitchen without showing her face. She had been a hippy in the sixties and didn't seem to have ever let go of it entirely. I liked her a lot and had no idea what to say to her.

'Er . . . Hi.' How she had come to produce a child like Simon I had no idea. Part of me wished my mother were more like Simon's, but for that to work, I would have to be, too. We were neither of us people persons. But you'd have to uncoil our DNA to fix that.

'Hey.' Simon's sister emerged from the kitchen, pursued by their cat, an enormous honey-coloured tom called Baggage. Sian was her mother's child for sure: long hair, flower-patterned hippy dress, easy smile, twelve going on twenty, zero interest in her brother or his strange collection of friends.

Stair-rods held the carpet on the stairs in Simon's house, and stylised tree patterns grew up the wallpaper, rising with you as you climbed. The place always had the same smell, a mix of lavender and sandalwood.

I'd been coming there since I was four. We'd been in the same kinder-garten, then the same primary school before both passing the exam for Maylert.

In the same period my parents had moved four times. Simon's house felt more constant than my own. More like my home than my home did.

'Here!' Simon held up an inch-high painted figure, a warrior with a war-hammer. I was to look, not touch.

'Sweet.' He had shown me how to do the magic he did with the brush. I couldn't do it.

On the table in his room half a dozen more figures stood ready for inspection beside a stack of rulebooks. A bright scattering of polyhedral dice and several incomplete map sheets completed the ensemble. People saw all that paraphernalia and their brains would dial in what they knew about games, board games with dice. Only this had monsters thrown in. Judgement made. But Dungeons & Dragons was never a board game. The figures and maps were just props. The rules weren't even called rules; they were guidebooks, handbooks, manuals. It was all there to give just enough structure to our shared imagination that we could vanish into it for hours, unwinding a story as we went. A story unique to us, filled with our own wonders, ingenuity, and proxy bravery. And it was something that carried on week after week, building over years even, creating a shared history, bonds that weren't ever going to appear across a Monopoly board or game of cards.

I went to my chair, finding for a moment that the room had grown distant, Simon's voice faint. Déjà vu gripped me. My encounter with Ian Rust had managed to push out the thoughts that had been spi-ralling through my sleepless mind. The hand that reached forward to lift the gaming mat didn't seem to be my own. The table before me became overlaid with my own hospital-vision of that same table the week before. My fingers remembered gripping the pen, grinding its point through the varnish, sending a message to myself . . . 'Nothing!' The wood lay smooth, undamaged.

'What?' Simon looked up from his monologue and blinked.

'Did . . . Was there something written here? Did you turn the table around?'

Another blink. 'No. What are you on about?'

'Nothing.' I let the mat flop back down. 'Just . . . Nothing.' It had seemed so real, but I guess that's the point about hallucinations. William of Ockham wasn't the first to point out, centuries ago, that the simplest answer is probably the right one, but he's the most famous. I was in hospital being poisoned. Which was more likely, some weird kind of time travel, or drug-induced hallucination? I snorted at myself.

'We miss something?' John pushed the door open.

Elton followed in, already pulling his books from his bag. 'I hope you guys were prayin', cos I'm bringing the pain today!' As the game master he was nominally in charge, designing the world we adventured in, but how we met those challenges was down to us.

Mia came in a second later, dark eyes ringed with black eyeliner, shooting me a look from beneath a black fringe. I blinked my surprise. One visit to the D&D table was unusual for any girl. Coming back for seconds was unheard of in my limited experience.

Elton arranged himself on the far side of the table, arraying his books as a shield for the notes and maps we weren't to see. He set out his dice, hands thick-knuckled from years of karate punches. The game master has to be the main creative force, something of an actor to portray those who populate his world, and an authoritative judge to settle player squabbles and end objections.

John sat to my right, annoyingly blonde and chiselled. Money, charm, and looks. Two out of three might be forgivable, but the whole set is bound to breed a little resentment. He ignored the character sheet before him and sat smiling at Mia. She ignored him, poring over her character sheet instead. She seemed to have rewritten the character Elton gave her the last time.

Simon's mum breezed in with a tray of orange juice and biscuits, followed by Baggage. She opened the window a crack.

'Mum!' Simon frowned at her. 'It's arctic out there.'

'A little fresh air is good for you.' She walked to the door. 'And I'm thinking of Mia. After a few hours with four boys in it, this room's a health hazard. Light a match and . . . boom!' She mimed the explosion with her hands, grinned, and walked off, the cat trailing in her wake.

'You feeling better?' Mia looked my way, but I still took a moment to understand that she was talking to me.

'Uh, yeah,' I lied.

'Better?' Simon shot me a dark look as if I'd betrayed him by consorting with the enemy.

'Nicodemus ate something that disagreed with him.' John mimed an exaggerated vomit. 'Or disagreed with something and then ate it.'

'I'm fine.' Nicodemus was my character's name. So perhaps I wasn't that imaginative after all.

'You better be.' Elton scowled over his defensive wall of books. He might be fearless in a fight and ready to punch out any number of Michael Devises, but when it came to illness he was as paranoid as they come.

'Well, if you start feeling sick, let me know.' Mia grinned. She pointed to her character sheet. 'It says here I have a "cure disease" spell. One size fits all, apparently. From little sniffles to leprosy.'

That would be nice. I muttered something about being fine. Mia had been given a cleric to play. Every newbie gets to play a cleric. They're the holy men, the priests, and they're stuck with the healing magic, which means they're always in demand after the battles but rarely during them. Mia had made hers a woman, a priestess of the Man Jesus, close enough to Catholic to make me think she had a grudge against them. Elton had mentioned something about her escaping a church school at some point, pursued by nuns.

It turns out that a shared imaginary crisis is a great icebreaker. By lunchtime, Elton had us running in panic from a collapsing cave system, and Mia and I were bickering like old friends over the relative merits of our survival plans. Even Simon found his voice, urging us to shut up and run!

An hour later, our small group of adventurers was advancing along a narrow forest path as the sun sank in the west.

'I'll climb a tree. A tall one. Maybe I can see an edge.' Simon gathered his dice. He played a thief with considerable acrobatic skills. When he said things like 'I'll climb a tree', imagination had to kick into a higher gear. In real life Simon had trouble climbing stairs.

'The tallest are smooth elms,' Elton said. 'Super hard to climb. Three skill checks. Roll seventeen or under.'

'So, a sixty-one per cent chance of making the top.' Simon gathered the dice.

'Woah!' Mia looked up. 'You just worked that out. Just like that?'

'He's a human calculator,' John said. 'Watch. Six hundred and eight times two hundred and thirty-seven?'

'A hundred and forty-four thousand and ninety-six,' Simon said without pausing, and rolled the dice.

'That's incredible!' Mia blinked.

'Not really. I was more likely to reach the top than fall,' Simon said.

'I mean the maths!'

Simon shrugged. 'Any pocket calculator can do the same.' He glanced my way. 'Nick's the genius. I'm going to read mathematics at

Cambridge. Nick knows that stuff already from his dad's books. I'm just good with numbers. Nick's off the scale.'

'Your dad's a mathematician?' Mia turned my way.

'Was. He died.'

Mia pressed her lips together in a moment's sympathy, then pushed on. 'If you're this wonder-boy, how come you're not at university already?'

'When they test him, he pretends he can't do it.' Simon looked at Elton. 'So? What do I see from my treetop?'

'Not a lot, man. It's getting dark. The sun's sinking in the treeline and everything's black and crimson. But it looks as if the forest ends some miles to the north.' Elton reached over to sketch an edge to the forest on our map.

Back on the forest track we pressed on, taking the northward choice when the trail forked. We tried lighting lanterns.

'The flame doesn't want to take.' Elton rolled some hidden dice. 'Like the night just eats it.'

'I'll cast a light spell.' My character, Nicodemus, studied the arcane; a trainee wizard, if you like.

Another hidden roll. 'You cast it and the trail lights up, but it's not like it should be, not like daylight, but as if you had a ten-watt bulb instead of a hundred. And it flickers at the edges. You can feel the darkness pushing on your spell like a physical pressure. It's slowly closing you down.'

'So, I grit my teeth and concentrate on keeping the spell going.'

'Okaaaaay . . . you can keep it at ten watts, but you're hurting, man. It's like a twisting in your guts. Pains shooting along your arms and legs.' Elton rolled another die. 'So you walk on. And on. It's only about five miles, but the tracks keep petering out and the wood's too thick to press through. You keep doubling back and trying new ways. It takes the whole night. Nicodemus is hurting bad by the time the trees start to thin, but you make it. The trail leads down to a brook. It's still inky, but dawn isn't far off.'

'Any bridge?' Simon asked.

'A brook. A few yards wide. You could jump it. Not in armour, but your thief could jump it from a standing start.' Elton rolled another die. 'Wandering monster!' Another roll and he gave a low whistle, eyes widening.

'Shit.' Wandering monsters are an unscripted part of the game – people, creatures, or even events that have a small chance of showing up each day and are selected at random from a big chart. I guess Ian Rust had been mine for the day. We never had any luck with them.

'Nicodemus sees it first. Back on the trail among the trees. A dark figure. A human, or human shaped. Just the starlight gleaming on a bald skull.'

'Wait . . .' I held my hand up, looking at John and Mia. 'You guys told him, right?'

'Told me what?' Elton looked up from his list of monsters. He seemed innocent enough, but then every game master has to be a bit of an actor.

'A dark forest. I'm sick. A brook. Not a river, but a brook. And then this shit with the bald guy.' I gave John a hard stare.

'Hey!' The realisation dawned on his face. 'We *did* this!'

I turned to Mia. '*You* told him then.' Not a question.

'It was a secret? Nobody said it was.' She shrugged and examined her character sheet. 'But no, actually. I didn't.'

'What the hell you all talking about?' Elton's brow furrowed in one of his famous frowns. I swear you could wedge pennies in those furrows and they'd stick.

'This is like what happened to us last night,' John said.

'You met a damn vampire last night?'

'Wait! What? This is a vampire? You're shitting me.' John sat up.

'We're dead.' Simon sighed and turned his character sheet over.

'You got a bad roll.' Elton lifted his books to show the dice. Double zero. A one-in-a-hundred chance. 'A very bad roll.'

'Still,' Mia said, 'at least you accidentally gave away what it is.'

Elton sniffed. 'You're a cleric. Priests can sense that sort of thing. It's undead. Can't hide that from a woman of the cloth.' He looked around the table. 'What do you do?'

'Run, of course!' I moved my wizard figure to the front of our group. 'It can eat the guys in armour!'

We all reached the same conclusion in short order and our brave band was soon pounding along the riverbank in terror.

'You're all strung out: Nicodemus in the lead, Fineous the thief just behind, the other two panting along some way back.' Elton arranged the figures. 'In the bend of the brook ahead of you—'

'Meander,' Simon interrupted.

'What?'

'When a river wriggles about like you've drawn . . . that's a meander.'

'OK, private school. In the *meander* ahead of you . . . the vampire is waiting. These guys can fly, you know.'

'Damn. I . . . Uh.' I looked down at my useless spells. 'I prepare to die.' Even if the vampire didn't kill us, just its touch could suck away experience, taking memories from a person, leaving them reduced, a shadow of what they were.

'Can't I drive it off?' Mia asked. 'Priests can do that, right?'

'Show him your cross!' John urged.

'I'm furious, but I don't see how that will help.' Mia grinned.

'No, he means—'

'She knows what he means, Simon.' Sometimes Simon could be slow with jokes.

Elton looked at the table in his rulebook. 'Clerics can turn undead away, but at your level . . . with a vampire . . .' He set two dice before her. 'Roll. It's going to take something extraordinary, though.'

'I'm all about extraordinary.' Mia tossed the dice with none of the puffing and agonising we always made over important rolls.

'Ninety-nine!'

'Holy crap.'

'OK, so you arrive just as the vamp's about to get a taste of Nicodemus here, and hold your cross up. It seems the Man Jesus is watching, and the crucifix starts to glow. Our bald friend staggers back before you, but . . . and this is the kicker, because you were never in any danger . . . the sucker can't pass over running water, so he's trapped. Of course, you guys could have waded over to safety at any time.'

'I knew that,' said Simon.

'I know you did,' said Elton. 'But knowing a thing and employing that knowledge when it's useful. Those aren't the same things.'

'He's trapped?' Mia asked.

'For as long as you can hold that cross up.'

'I think I can hold it until the sun rises.' Mia grinned.

'Damn, she's right.' John leaned back from the table. 'You, Mia, just killed yourself a vampire!'

'Well, sheeeiit . . .' Elton shook his head. 'He don't plead or nothing. He just watches you all like you're bits of tasty meat.'

'Don't look at his eyes,' Simon said. 'They can hypnotise.'

Elton huffed. 'At least you remembered that. So, you wait until the sun's rays touch him and he screams and turns to dust, all in a moment; just his clothes falling down where he stood.' He shook his head again. 'Now tell me *that* happened last night! I dare you.'

'Well, the running did.' John grinned. 'And he could have been a vampire . . .'

'I check the remains. He's got to have treasure. Right?' Simon played a greedy thief pretty well when it came down to it.

Elton returned to his charts. 'I gotta roll that up. Take five.'

I stood and stretched sore legs. I went to the window. It was only open half an inch, but the cold air had been playing on my neck, making my bones ache. I was reaching to close it when I saw him. 'No. He wasn't a vampire.' None of them heard me. I knew that the bald man from the park wasn't a vampire, though. He was standing there in the sunshine. Admittedly, weak January sunshine, but enough to dust a vampire. He looked up at me over the fence at the back of Simon's garden, watching from the street.

CHAPTER 4

'You good for Saturday?' Simon stopped me in the hall between maths and French. He always talked about our D&D sessions with the intensity the first team rugby coach reserved for grudge matches. As if missing one would be a matter of life and death.

'Yeah, I'll be there.'

'Will Elton be bringing . . . you know?'

'Mia? You can say her name, Si. You won't summon her.'

Simon gave a nervous grin and glanced over his shoulder as if she might be there. 'Yes. Her.'

'She's alright. Saved our bacon with the vamp.' I wanted her to be there.

'She's with Elton? Right?'

'Nah.' I grinned. 'They're just mates. Fancy your chances, Si?' Elton seemed to have a dozen girls who were friends, but girlfriends were never mentioned. Odd, because in school we talked about girls all the time. At least imaginary ones. Maybe it was only a boys' school habit. Perhaps that went away when you had enough of the real thing around you. 'Mia is cute, though. But I think John might just have the upper hand in that game, Simon, old boy.'

Simon coloured. 'How about your stalker? He going to show, too?'

My sighting of the 'stalker' had ended our last session somewhat abruptly. He'd been walking away by the time I got the others to the window, and a hurried mass exit into the street hadn't been hurried enough to catch him. Much of that was down to me having come over kind of spacey at the window, like I was drowning in déjà vu. Going down the stairs I got this weird vision of me coming up them that morning, and in the confusion managed to fall down the last dozen steps. So our prey made a clean escape. Not that I knew what we would have done if we had caught him.

John had laughed after and said that he couldn't have picked the park guy from a line-up at the gates while he was still sweating from running after Mia and me. So how I could be so sure it was the same man, he didn't know. 'It's not like there aren't a lot of bald guys around . . .'

But Mia had been more pensive. She'd been first to join me at the window. She only saw him walking away, but even so . . . 'There was something about him, though.'

The hall was clearing as each classroom sucked in its allotted students. 'We gotta go.'

Simon and I joined the end of the queue shuffling into the French lesson. Not one of my strong subjects.

'Were we supposed to be having a test today? Because I didn't—'

'You moulting, Hayes?' Someone flicked the back of my head. 'It's all over your shoulders.'

I turned to find Michael Devis behind me, a tuft of black hair between his finger and thumb, held out as if it were something distasteful.

'Losing your hair at your age, Hayes? Is that what happens to nerds?' He let the tuft drop.

Michael Devis had a broad face, dark flinty eyes, and a remarkably clear complexion for a fifteen-year-old boy. He deserved acne. You want people's badness to show. The poison inside him should be bursting out. Instead, he looked almost amiable when he wasn't sneering. I was taller than him, but he filled his blazer out in that chunky sort of way that's part muscle and part fat. 'What?' he asked, the sneer deepening into threat.

But the falling hair had taken my attention. A thick dark tuft. The kind you should have to rip out. They said that if the chemo was going to take your hair it would do it somewhere between the second and third week. I wondered if eight days were a record.

I came to Simon's house the next day wearing a woollen hat. Not one of those colourful things with a bobble, but a thin black one my dad once took skiing before he realised he couldn't ski and would never learn. It was the kind of cool hat New Order would wear . . . if they wore stupid woolly hats.

'Vampires carry class H treasure.' Simon opened the door practically as I reached for it and began talking. 'With the right rolls, this could be a gold mine for us.'

I followed him up the stairs.

'Hey, Nicko! Nice hat!' Simon's mum, milk bottles chinking as she carried them to the front door.

Even with that hint Simon remained oblivious. I could have come in wearing a full Mickey Mouse suit and I doubt he would have commented.

'What's with the hat?' John walked in before I'd finished getting my books on the table.

'Religious thing. I'll tell you all about it at the end of the session.'

'No, really. What's with the hat? Is it lined with tinfoil?'

'Seriously.' I lifted my hands. 'End of the session. All will be revealed!'

'Bad haircut.' John nodded to Simon, who was blinking at the offending item of clothing as if it had been a state secret up until this point.

We went through the same process when Elton and Mia arrived, but Simon proved to be the driving force that moved us on past the sartorial issues, motivated by avarice. 'I've been waiting a week to see what this pile of dust was carrying. I don't care if Nick has grown horns. Tell me!'

Elton settled to business. 'Well, there's a leather pouch with fifty gold ducats in it, and a ruby about the size of your thumbnail.'

'Fifty gold. Medium ruby. Check.' Simon wrote it down on his personal treasure list, ever the thief. 'C'mon, there has to be more than that.'

'And an iron tube, a foot long, two inches in diameter, worked like coiling ivy, capped at both ends.'

'Scroll case. Check. What else?'

'That's it.' Elton leaned back in his chair, hands behind his head.

'Damnation!' The closest Simon came to swearing, though his mum could make sailors blush.

'What's on the scroll?' Mia asked. Her cleric could cast spells, and a scroll in a posh case was most often going to be an enchantment.

'You open the case. There's a hiss as the stopper comes loose, like someone sucking air over their teeth, and a smell . . . a kind of dry bones smell that makes you want to stop breathing. You fish out a scroll of thick, yellowed parchment. It looks suspiciously like human skin and you're kinda glad you're wearing gloves.' Elton conjured the vision. 'The letters have been branded into the parchment, maybe while it was still someone's skin. It hurts your eyes to look at them and none of it makes any sense.'

'Some bad juju here.' John reached out to edge his warrior away from Mia's cleric.

'Give it to Nicodemus,' Simon said. 'Whatever it is, it's not holy.'

I nodded. 'I'll give it a try.' I held up my hand before Elton could open his mouth. 'I'll put on some gloves.'

Elton shrugged. 'So you study it. The letters make a kind of sense to you. It's the style of magic you practise, but way above your pay grade. It's so difficult to understand that it starts to give you the headache from hell.'

'I sit down and press on with it. The others can wait.' My character had maximum intelligence. A kind of conceit since it rarely mattered beyond a certain level.

'OK. Well, you can only just understand it.' Elton reached out and gave me a folded piece of paper so I would know what the spell was and could choose to share the knowledge with the others or not. I read it and handed it back.

'The lamest spell in the game,' I said. 'Power Word Kill.'

John frowned, Mia looked blank, Simon inhaled. 'In what universe is Power Word Kill lame? It's a ninth-level spell! We could sell that scroll for thousands!'

'What does it do?' Mia asked.

'You speak one word and point at someone,' Simon said. 'They die. Then the scroll turns to dust.'

'See what I mean?' I asked.

'You can kill *anyone*?' John's frown deepened.

'Well, any person or creature we've met in the game so far, yes.'

'Just like that? No saving throw?'

'Yes.'

'That *is* lame.' John nodded.

'It's brilliant!' Simon said.

'Why don't you like it, Nick?' Mia tilted her head to one side, watching me. I found that I liked her attention.

'Pretty much everything that happens in this game gives you a chance. You get a saving throw, or some other roll of the dice, and if you get a good enough result you can wriggle out from under. It might be an impossible ask. One chance in twenty. One in a hundred. But you get a chance. Not a choice, but a chance. This, though? Nothing. The person with the spell says "die", and you do. End of story.' I shrugged. 'I don't like that.'

Mia pursed her lips, then nodded. 'I get it.'

The game moved on, with the scroll tucked into Nicodemus's backpack: too valuable to use and still a bone of contention around the table. Hours rolled past, as they do when you're wholly occupied with something. The real world took a seat at the back and Elton's imaginary one held centre stage.

Mia proved to be funny, shockingly rude on occasion, and the sneaky kind of clever that gets things done. I found myself stealing glances at her. She threw herself into the game in a way that I still couldn't, without reservation. I wanted to be more like her. If I was going to die young, I wanted to at least squeeze the juice out of life rather than pick at it. But you can't change who you are. Not even with a gun to your head.

'You OK, Nick?' Mia, pausing with the dice ready to throw. 'You look pale.'

'All good.' I waved her on. The pain in my leg eased for a moment.

In hospital they ask you to rate your discomfort on a scale of ten. I guess it's the best they can come up with, but it fails to capture the nature of the beast. Pain can stay the same while you change around it. And, like a thumb of constant size, what it blocks out depends on how close it gets to you. At arm's length a thumb obscures a small fragment of the day. Held close enough to your eye it can blind you to everything that matters, relegating the world to a periphery. Playing the game kept my mind on something else. For most of the session, the pains in the long bones of my legs and the sickness in my stomach subsided to annoyance. At other times, they were a spike pinning me to the fact of my disease.

'So . . .' Elton closed his notebook and scooped up his dice. 'That's all got to keep for another day, 'cause I'm out of here.' He started to pile rulebooks into his bag. 'All we got to know now is, how come the hat, Nicky? How come the hat?' A broad grin.

And suddenly all eyes were on me. There had been times at the table that I'd forgotten I was wearing the hat. All at once it felt heavy. I had considered lying. Just telling them that it was hair loss due to anxiety. Stress alopecia they called it. I looked it up. But although I felt a wholly unwarranted degree of shame in admitting to cancer, it seemed somehow worse to declare myself to be going bald at fifteen without good reason.

'Yeah, what about the hat, Nick?' Mia asked, smiling.

My mouth went dry, and suddenly out of nowhere I was struggling to keep my voice steady. As if I might burst into tears at any moment or something equally stupid. 'I didn't come to school this Thursday, or last, because I was on an oncology ward.'

'Onk-what-ogy?' John snorted.

'Ward?' Simon frowned. 'Like a hospital.'

'Cancer.' A scowl from Elton. 'Not cool, dude. That shit's not funny. Don't joke about it.'

I paused. Even while sat there trying to get the words out without my voice breaking I was struck by the fact that each of them had said almost exactly what they said in my weird hospital vision.

'I'm not joking.' I pulled my cap off.

Silence. Just the four of them staring at my white scalp showing through thinning black hair.

Elton was the first to speak. 'No, man . . .' He stood from his chair, dark eyes glistening. 'This ain't right.'

'Cancer?' Simon, quiet, not looking up.

'Not while I'm in charge.' Against all expectations, Elton came round the table in three strides and literally dragged me out of my seat into a hug. I hadn't been hugged by a boy before. Or a girl, come to think of it. Just Mother on rare occasions, and my two grandmothers at Christmases. I stood there, not knowing what to do with my arms, jaw locked tight against any outburst of emotion.

'Shit.' John realised he should say something, his face in motion as if unable to find the right expression. 'I . . . Well . . . Shit!' He thumped the table hard enough to make the dice dance and the figures fall over. 'They're going to make you better, though, right?'

'Sure.' I eased myself from Elton's embrace. 'We live in an age of miracles, don't we? I've got a computer in my bedroom! Well . . . a Commodore 64 . . .' I realised I was babbling. 'I, uh. I gotta go.'

I started to stuff my papers and books into my bag. Nothing wanted to fit, everything at awkward angles. 'You OK, Si?'

Simon kept his gaze on the table, brow twisted in furious concentration like when he totally disagreed with one of the game master's rulings and was building up the head of steam required for him to object.

'Si?' He was chewing his cheek. Always a bad sign. 'Earth to Simon?' I reached for his shoulder.

'Cancer?' He launched himself to his feet, scattering two chairs. 'Cancer!' A shout that had footsteps running up the stairs. 'What the hell were you thinking?' Red-faced and furious. I'd only seen him like it once, years back when we teased him past breaking point on some small thing. Although he was short, Simon was almost as wide as he was tall, and when he barrelled at you there was no stopping him. 'You're ruining everything!' Tears now, glistening on scarlet cheeks. I couldn't blame him. A large part of me wanted to shout and cry and throw things about, too. But if I broke that dam open and let those emotions flow, I had no idea how I could close it again. Instead, I rammed the last few things into my bag.

'What's going on?' Simon's mum in the doorway, an apron on, hands still soapy from the dishes.

'I've got to go.' I snatched my bag and squeezed past her, everyone talking at once. 'Sorry.'

'Nick? Nicko!'

I made it down the stairs despite nearly tripping over Baggage and ending my dramatic exit in Accident and Emergency. A moment later I was out in the street, running.

I always felt I should be good at running. Skinny. Long legs. But no. Whatever plumbing of heart and lungs is needed for the long-distance runner . . . well, I have the other sort. Two blocks from Simon's house, I was doubled up, leaning on a gate post, gasping for breath. A cough, and suddenly the gasping turned into retching, and I was splattering the pavement with a mixture of chocolate digestives and orange juice.

I clung to the gate, lines of drool hanging from my open mouth, deep in misery. I couldn't blame Simon. He wasn't wired like regular people, and it went beyond the pocket calculator in his head. He couldn't deal with change. Even good change was bad. And bad change . . . well, that could make him lose it.

'Jesus, Hayes! The fuck you doin'?'

It seemed so far beyond reasonable that Michael Devis should happen upon me in that moment that I ignored the voice and kept my head down.

'That's disgusting. Messing up the street.'

I wiped my mouth, continuing to ignore him.

'Heard you bumped into Ian Rust the other day. Chucked your shit in the gutter.'

I straightened up, trembling, though whether from fear, anger, or puking I couldn't tell.

'I should empty your crap on that lot.' Devis nodded to the glistening mess at my feet. He was just starting to reach for the sports bag on my shoulder when someone came past me. A dark figure. And, in the same motion, swung a fist right into Devis's mouth. A real haymaker punch.

Devis staggered back clutching his face, then fell on his arse. He groaned and his hands came away scarlet from his mouth. The newcomer loomed over him. My first thought had been that Elton had caught up with us, but it was the bald guy.

'You better run, because I enjoyed that and want to do it again.' He kicked Devis's outstretched foot. 'Scram!'

Devis got to his feet, clutching his face again, half-dazed. The man took a quick step forward and Devis turned to run.

'You're a fucking nutter.' He got to the corner. 'I'll have the police on you, you bastard!'

The man made to run after him and Devis took off.

'Wow, that felt good!' The man turned back to me. 'I've been waiting twenty-five years to do that.' He shook his hand. 'Hurt like fuck, though!'

I stood for a moment, mouth open, finding no words. He was tall, a couple of inches taller than me, six two, six three maybe. Not properly old. Forty perhaps. Something about him looked disturbingly familiar.

'Who . . . ? Why . . . ?' I felt dizzy. The times I'd seen the man before all tried to crowd in on me at once. At the hospital, the park, the window. I reached for the wall, needing support. 'Why did you do that?'

'Why?' He flexed his hand, winced, then grinned. 'To gain your trust, of course.'

CHAPTER 5

'He what?'

'Punched Michael Devis square in the mouth.'

'No way?' John stood up from the end of my bed as if the idea was too much to take sitting down. 'I saw him today in school. The side of his face is all purple.'

'Good. He deserves it.'

'Still . . .' John sat down again. I winced. 'The guy's bat-shit crazy, right?'

'Off the scale.' I pushed a stray sweater over the pile of quantum mechanics books on my bedside table.

'Well, if you're going to have a stalker, then that's the type to have: A Devis-thumping one.' John shook his head and looked around my room. The bed took half the space. John's bedroom was the size of a barn and filled with cool stuff. He had a Viking battle-axe on his wall, and a Syrian helm with a chainmail coif on a stand. 'You coming back to school this week?'

'Maybe on Friday.' I shrugged.

'Did he look crazy? I mean close up. Twitchy?'

'Uh. Not really.' He'd looked like my father. It wasn't him. There were enough differences for that to be clear even if the funeral didn't settle the matter. But he had looked enough like him to be a secret uncle I'd never been told about.

'What did he say?'

'Crazy stuff. Weird things.' He told me that we would speak again in a week. He'd said something about needing time for the echoes to settle before we could talk properly. I'd been hurting and disoriented, so I couldn't remember everything. He told me his name, though: Demus.

'I'm Demus, you're Nick.' The bald guy had raised a hand to ward off questions. 'I know everything . . . We'll talk next week when you're ready to listen. Until then, why not stay off school and do your homework?'

'Homework?' I'd echoed stupidly.

'Bone up on quantum mechanics. Particularly Everett's many-world interpretation. You can get the books at the Imperial College library. Speak to Professor James in the maths department. Show him that thing with knots in n-space topologies. He'll like that.'

'How do you—'

'I know everything. I just told you that. Tell Mother you're sick and can't go to school. It's not like she can argue with that.' He'd reached out to press a piece of folded paper into my hand. 'And memorise these numbers. That's the most important part.'

'Uh?' I looked at the white square in my palm.

'When the time comes, make a show of it. You need to get the others on board.' And with that he had hurried off back the way he came. I'd taken a few steps after him, but another bout of nausea brought me to my knees, and when it let me go Demus was gone.

'Nick?' John snapped his fingers in front of my face.

'W . . . what?'

'Spaced out on me there, buddy.'

'Sorry. Just tired, I guess.' I'd been up late, reading.

'Yeah.' John stood again. 'Look, I better go. Don't want to wear you out. I already had the lecture from your mum!' He picked up his school briefcase. 'Mia was asking about you, you know?'

'You called her?' It was stupid, but I didn't want John talking to her. She had been out of my league even before I started vomiting and shedding, and I hadn't got a clue what I would do even if John stepped back and waved me on. But still. Even though he was my friend, a small mean voice complained that he already had every good thing. Mia shouldn't be on his list of acquisitions, too.

'*She* called *me*!' He grinned, showing perfect white teeth that I felt an unaccountable urge to punch. 'Anyway. Gotta go. And you, you have to show on Saturday or we'll all come here and crowd in like sardines.' He got up, then paused at the door. 'Oh, I almost forgot. You'll like this one. In other news: Ian Rust got himself expelled! Devis won't know what to do with himself with his mentor gone.'

'Expelled?' That really did bring a smile to my face. 'What did he do?'

John frowned at that. 'Twisted David Steiner's arm up behind his back so far that something snapped.'

'Something?' My stomach went cold.

'A bone.'

'And nobody tried to stop him?'

'Mr Roberts did. But Rust just broke Steiner's arm anyway, and then pulled a knife on Roberts.'

'Holy crap! Rust's a fucking lunatic.' Mr Roberts was a PE teacher, over six feet tall and packed with muscle.

'Indeed.' John nodded. 'The police were called, but Rust had vanished by the time they came. Besides, they won't hold him, just set a court date or something . . .'

When John had gone I turned on my reading lamp and returned to my textbooks. It was that or go downstairs to watch *Dallas* with Mother. She said it was her guilty pleasure, and it was true that it was about the only programme that would convince her to watch something other than BBC2. Even the instigation of a fourth channel hadn't managed to do that!

I had to admit that quantum mechanics was clever stuff. Most of it danced to its own tune, but there was still enough fundamental mathematics underlying all the pretty manipulations to keep me interested.

I'd done what Demus said to do. After all, he had driven his fist into Devis's over-loud mouth for me. And what else was there to do? I'd been presented with a mystery. I could focus on that, or I could worry about leukaemia chewing its way through the marrow of my bones. No contest really. Quantum mechanics wasn't exactly easy, but it unravelled itself a lot more willingly than the strangeness that Demus constituted. Who the hell was he? Why had he singled me out? And why now?

Getting off school was easy. Escaping the house, harder. I'd taken the tube to South Kensington and hobbled my way past the Natural History Museum to Imperial College, an ugly set of buildings poured out of concrete mixers in the sixties, right behind the Royal Albert Hall.

I'd tried to get into the library first, picking up a leaflet from the main reception, but was escorted from the premises by an efficient woman with grey-streaked hair scraped into a tight bun and those angular glasses that they must force librarians to wear. Apparently, teenagers in Joy Division T-shirts were not welcome, and I should be in school. Though how she could distinguish me from the students, I didn't know. And what kind of rowdy youth plays truant to come to a university physics library?

Professor James had seemed rather surprised to see me at his door. He asked me if I were lost. I answered by asking him if he had considered the Ryberg Hypothesis in non-Euclidian manifolds above five dimensions, because it suddenly became provable, and that fact had powerful implications for high order knot theory. After that, he was all mine.

To me the most interesting thing was, for once, not about the mathematics, but about the fact that Demus had known both that I was aware of the professor's work in the area, and that I'd made several advances on what James had published.

'This is quite extraordinary, young man.' The professor sat down heavily, leaning back from our pages of scribbling. He had a habit of tugging at himself when he concentrated and now looked as if he'd been pulled backwards through a hedge. 'Nicholas Hayes, did you say?'

'Nick.'

He pulled at the corner of his moustache. 'No relation to Alfred Hayes, of course?'

'My father.'

'Ah . . .' He seized at that like a drowning man. 'This is his unpublished work? I must say, I'm tremendously impressed that you understand any of it, Nick. What are you, first year, second?'

'Actually, I'm not at the university yet. Which, uh, brings me to the real reason for my visit. I need to borrow your library card. Also, if you could call down to the librarian to expect me, that would help a lot.'

All I had to do was promise to come back with any more of my father's papers that I might find, and Professor James couldn't get his card into my hands quickly enough.

'Nick?' A knock at my bedroom door. I lifted my head from *Quantum Mechanics and Path Integrals* by Richard Feynman, the world's greatest living expert on the subject. Another knock. I had the feeling there might have been several already that I failed to notice.

'Yes?'

Mother opened the door. 'You have another visitor.' She sounded a little odd.

'Hi, Nick!' Mia squeezed past Mother, who had positioned herself as guardian of the doorway. 'I bought chocolate brazils. They're kinda like grapes. Only chocolate, and . . . not.' She put the box beside me on the bed.

'Uh . . .' I blinked up at her. She wasn't in uniform. I'd assumed she went to Elton's school, but had never asked. Instead, she was gothed-up to eleven: black, black, more black, and some zips; black-circled eyes in a white face, lips a very dark red. 'Hi.'

Mother stayed where she was, her smile fixed in that way we Brits use to show we wholly disapprove of something.

'Hi.' I said it again because suddenly it was all I had. I also became painfully aware that my woolly hat was just beyond arm's reach, and that putting it on now would be too obvious. Instead, I had to treat her to the full patchwork horror show of my scalp.

'Hi,' Mia said. And then, just as I thought we might be locked in this death-spiral of greeting for the rest of our lives, 'What you reading?'

Instead of answering, I looked pointedly over her shoulder at Mother, who had already outstayed the sociably acceptable linger limit by a factor of at least three. 'I'd love a drink, Mum.'

She missed a beat at 'Mum' but rallied herself admirably. 'Orange ju—'

'Tea, please.' I'd never asked for tea before.

'Of course.' Her smile re-fixed itself. 'And . . . Mia? Would you like some . . . tea?'

'Coffee, if you have it.' Mia smiled. 'White with two sugars.'

Mother retreated. I waited until I heard her footsteps on the stairs.

'Quantum mechanics.' I held up the book.

'Cool.' Mia sat on the bed. Closer than friends normally sit next to friends. She smelled of patchouli oil. I liked it. 'What's that about then?'

'Well . . . it's about everything, really. It's the most accurate and complete description of the universe we've ever had. It's also completely

51

bonkers.' I hesitated. I was pretty sure this wasn't what you were supposed to talk about when girls came to visit.

'More bonkers than general relativity?' Mia took the book from the death grip I had it in. 'The twins paradox is hard to beat.'

With a sigh, I relaxed. She was one of us! The magical power of D&D to draw together people who knew things. Who cared about questions that didn't seem to matter.

'Way weirder.' Mia was right, the twins paradox was hard to beat. When Einstein showed the world that time was made of rubber and could be stretched for one person and squeezed for another until their lives were years out of kilter . . . that had been pretty strange. But even Einstein had balked at the cosmic strangeness quantum mechanics throws at us. 'I've been looking at the many worlds interpretation.'

Mia started to open the box of chocolate brazils. 'Go on.'

'Well. The thing is, quantum mechanics is chock full of crazy, but every prediction it makes is perfect to as many decimal places as we can measure. Loads of our technology is built on it. Consequently, we just have to swallow the madness.'

'Right.' Mia pushed a chocolate past her lips, then offered the box to me.

'What helps a bit is that you can move the crazy around depending on how you interpret the theory. None of the predictions change, and the crazy doesn't go away: it's just that the mad thing you're asked to accept as the price of entry changes.'

'And many worlds is one price? What does it mean?' She bit off half the casing from her second brazil with small white teeth, exposing the nut.

'It applies whenever *any* choice is made. You can think of those choices as you choosing to stay in or go out, but it really means whenever anything that has multiple possible results happens. And it says that each time a choice is made the universe splits, and there is a universe in which each possible outcome happens. And those universes go on and

do their own sweet thing forever after without ever interacting again.'
I sketched a tree on the notepad beside me, explaining that the trunk
represented our timeline and that at each fork of the branches lay a deci-
sion, splitting the universe's timeline into multiple new timelines. At the
tips of the smallest twigs lay all the possible outcomes, a multitude of
timelines waiting to be split yet again by new choices. 'Basically, we're
all infinite.'

'Wow.' She sucked her fingers.

'Yeah . . .' I looked away from her red lips and tried to regain my
train of thought. 'So, there is a universe where Nick Hayes has rolled a
one every single time he ever threw a die. And a trillion others where he
hasn't. In that one universe he's probably famous and gets on TV shows.
And the thing is, it's just regular chance. Each time he rolls a six-sided
die again, he has exactly the same probability of getting a one as everyone else, and in five of the six branching universes, the TV hosts blink
and Nick says, "But . . . it always works . . . I don't understand . . ." But
in one of the six, Nick chalks up another victory and the world thinks
it's a trick or magic.'

'That's legitimately mad.' Mia nodded. 'So . . . in one universe,
one of my premium bonds wins the hundred-thousand-pound prize
tomorrow?'

'Yup. In fact, there will be a universe where *all* of your premium
bonds win a prize tomorrow . . . and then you're killed by a meteorite.'

I didn't even notice Mother come in to deliver the drinks. We talked
for an hour or more, physics mostly. It didn't matter to me that Mia had
probably come out of pity, and that if I weren't dying of leukaemia, she
wouldn't have come within a mile of me without John or Elton on her
arm. I just enjoyed being with her.

'I gotta go.' Mia glanced at her watch and brushed her hair out of
her eyes. She looked at the bedroom door that Mother had left decid-
edly ajar. 'I, uh, got you something else.' She kept her voice low and
placed a small black rectangle between us, wrapped in cling film. At

first, I thought it was a strange bar of chocolate. 'It's supposed to help with the pain and feeling sick.' She bit her lip. 'I read up on it.'

I wasn't a hundred per cent sure, but I thought it was probably cannabis resin. A lot of it. 'I . . . Thanks. But I don't—'

'I know you don't smoke.' She grinned. 'You faked it better than John, though!' The grin broadened. 'But you can eat it. Not more than this.' She showed half the nail of her little finger. 'Just thought it might help.'

I looked down at the rectangle. Then covered it with my hand as she withdrew hers. 'Thanks.'

'No problem.' She got up to go, stealing one last chocolate. 'Saturday.' She paused at the door. 'Or we all come here.'

CHAPTER 6

I made it to Simon's house on Saturday. Mother gave me a lift, which was nice of her because I don't think I could have walked it. My third round of chemo was really starting to bite. The resin helped, though it made Mother think I was more ill than I was. It also made concentrating on quantum mechanics textbooks difficult, so I took the minimum required to lift me far enough out of the pit to function, without going too high to care.

The night had been sleepless, adrift on a black sea of self-pity. And why not? I stared at the dark, one thought churning over the next. I'd always had the sense of a whole life ahead of me, an endless series of sunrises and sunsets. A decade seemed like forever, and it would take two of them just to reach the age my mother was right now. Cancer had closed that down. Like the big C, curling in on itself, my view of the future had narrowed to tunnel vision, aimed squarely at the next week, next month . . . would I have a next year? I was carrying not only the burden of my sickness but the pressure of making something worthwhile of each day now that my towering stack of them had fallen into ruin and left me clutching at each hour as it slipped between my fingers.

I sat yawning in the back of the car, like a kid, staring at Demus's note. It had two words on it and ten numbers. 'BATTER UP.' Written in crudely drawn capitals as if a child had done it. I'd memorised the numbers: 4, 17, 17, 6 . . . it went on. I tried to fix them in my mind. Simon could lock a sequence of numbers into his head at glance. I'd always struggled with memory. Phone numbers leaked out of me. So it was probably good I hadn't many friends. Understanding was a different matter. I could get an idea quick enough, but a list of numbers . . . even without the dope I'd be struggling.

Simon's mum greeted me at the door rather than Simon. She waved to Mother, still parked across the road, signalling in some universal mothering code that I was in good hands.

'The hat suits you.' She gave me an unexpected hug and aimed me upstairs. 'They're all here already.'

I winced my way up the stairs. On the oncology ward, I was still synchronised with talkaholic Eva. She continued vomiting like a puke-fountain, but in between she said she felt fine, and her dull brown hair was still clinging uninspiringly to her skull. Of all of them, I seemed to be winning the race to the bottom. The nurses tutted to themselves, the doctors puzzled over blood counts and clotting factors. The white walls and starched uniforms were failing me. Their poison was hurting me more than it was hurting the rogue cells filling my veins.

'Holy cornflakes! It's hat-man!' John raised his coke can in my direction. The table was decked out: dice ready, maps sorted, figures positioned.

'How you doing, Nick?' Elton got up as if I were an elderly relative who might need helping to my chair.

'Of all the worlds, in all the universes, he walks into mine.' Mia wrapped the *Casablanca* quote around Everett's many-world interpretation and gained yet another level in my esteem.

'You're late.' Simon didn't look up from his character sheet. I'd known him pretty much all my life. He was the way he was. So much of what he felt couldn't ever crystallise into something small enough for words or action. Instead it raced around in his skull, winding him tighter and tighter. I wouldn't ever know more than a fraction of what was going on with him, but I knew enough that we could be friends.

'Woah.' As I sat down, I saw Mia's black eye for the first time. 'What happened?'

'You should see the other guy.' She made an unconvincing smile.

'But what—'

'It's not important.' Mia looked pointedly at Elton, who frowned but took his cue and began the game.

'The fortress backs against a granite ridge. It's half-ruined now, but you can see that once it was magnificent. It covers acres. The morning sun's just starting to catch on the towers. Down below it's all shadows . . .'

The game went on its way, Elton's skill drawing us in and wrapping us in his imagination. The rest of the world faded into the background, taking most of my discomfort with it. Only the square of paper in my pocket kept me anchored to something outside the fortress we had to search.

Elton had us creeping through darkened halls hung with dead ivy, forcing ancient doors, descending into the subterranean levels below the vast fortifications. Hours slipped by. It was almost time to go before I knew it.

'The chamber's huge,' Elton said. 'You could drive a double decker bus through it, and there's shafts of light here and there from openings in the ceiling, leading up to the outside.'

'So, we're blind then,' Mia said.

John frowned. 'He just told us there's light.'

'Yeah, but like spotlights: patches of brightness that take away your night sight and hide what's in the shadows. And Simon's lantern isn't going to touch a place this big . . .'

'Fineous,' Simon muttered. He always wanted to be addressed by his character name in the game.

'Sorry.' Mia didn't look sorry. 'Alright, *Fineous*, how about you shoot an arrow or two out there and see what you stir up?'

Simon shrugged. 'I put my lantern to one side, get out my short bow and loose an arrow toward the back of the hall.'

'There's a cry of pain,' Elton said.

'Shit.' I moved Nicodemus behind the armoured bulk of John's warrior.

'Why shit?' he asked.

'He didn't roll,' I said. 'If Elton didn't roll to see if the arrow hit anyone . . .'

'That means the place is full of them!' Mia said.

'They come boiling out of the back of the hall.' Elton began gleefully advancing orc figures. 'Dozens of them. Big Uruk-Hai in chainmail, ogres, too.'

John moved his warrior behind my mage. 'Batter up! Time for a fireball!'

'What?' A cold finger of recognition ran down my spine.

'Fireball! Quick, before they're too near!'

'You said "batter up".' The words on Demus's piece of paper. Coincidence, surely?

John tapped his finger before the leading orcs. 'Come on, Nicodemus. Fireball! It's what we brought a mage with us for in the first place.'

I blinked. 'OK. I'll detonate it at the back of the hall.'

Elton nodded. 'Roll the damage.'

I picked up a six-sided die. If you asked the rest of them to roll six dice, they'd grab a handful. Me, I liked to do it one at a time. I tossed it out.

'Four.' Elton started to keep tally.

'I knew that . . .' The first number on Demus's note.

'Knew what?' Mia asked.

'That I was going to roll a four.'

'Big deal.' John snorted.

'No, really. I knew it was going to be a four.'

'If your party trick is guessing one of six numbers, then you need a new trick.' John picked up a twenty-sided die. 'Impress me, hat-man!'

'Seventeen,' I said, almost sure it wouldn't be.

John let the die go. A D20 is almost a ball. Technically it's an icosahedron, but it rolls like a ball. It kept going until it fetched up against Mia's newly acquired rulebook. 'Seventeen!' she exclaimed. 'Cool!'

'Yeah. Good guess.' John shrugged. 'Do it again.' And he set his other D20 rolling.

'Seventeen again,' I said.

And it was.

'Shit.' John sat up straight. 'What're the odds?'

'One in four hundred,' Simon answered, unimpressed. 'Get on and roll the damage.'

'Six,' I said, and tossed out another D6. It landed on six.

That gave even Simon pause. He gave me a flat look and scooped up three D12, clutching them in his fist. 'What will these be?'

'One, two, then eleven.'

Simon dropped them one after the other. One, two, then eleven.

'What are the odds now?' Mia breathed.

'One in four million, one hundred and forty-seven thousand, two hundred,' Simon said with a frown. 'Which means it's a trick. How are you doing this, Nick?'

I shrugged and tossed out three more six-sided dice. 'Three, five, three.' Then I took out Demus's piece of paper and unfolded it for them. The numbers were all there, written down in order.

'Do it again!' Elton demanded.

'I can't. That's all I've got.' I threw out the last die of the forgotten damage. 'Six,' I hoped. It was a four.

'All you've got?' Mia asked. 'I don't understand.'

'What's it say there?' Elton came round from the game master's side of the table, leaving the seat of his authority. He picked up the paper. 'Shit! *Batter up*. That's what you said, ain't it, John? Batter up? You in on this, too? All of you got weighted dice or some shit?' He snatched up the last couple of dice I'd thrown.

John leaned over to squint at the paper. 'Holy crap . . . I said that . . . You wrote it down just then!'

'How?' I shook my head. 'My stalker gave me that last Saturday.'

'This is nonsense.' Simon banged the table. 'This isn't real.'

It seemed a bold claim for someone who five minutes ago was wholly invested in blowing up orcs, but I had a lot of sympathy for his point of view. 'Look, I don't know how he did it.'

'The guy who hit Michael Devis . . . he knew what those dice would roll?' John ran his fingers into his hair, clutching his head as if he might squeeze some sense into the situation. 'You know this is all mental right?'

'I know.' It made having cancer seem almost everyday.

'So what do we do?' Elton asked.

'See if any of the orcs are still alive.' Simon tapped the table.

I ignored him. 'I don't know. What can we do?'

'Go out and find this guy!' Elton smacked fist into palm. 'And . . .'

'And what?' Mia stood up. 'Smack him around for knowing the future? Like that makes sense. Anyway . . . he'd know you were coming.'

'Nick!' Simon's mum calling up the stairs. 'Your mother just went by, looking for a parking space.'

'I better go.' I started heaping stuff into my bag. I had plenty of time. Mother was a terrible parker and the roads round Simon's were always jammed. But I wanted to be out of there. I felt sick again, and I wanted space for my own astonishment, rather than demands from the rest of them that I sort out their disbelief.

A few moments later, I was hobbling down the stairs. Behind me, John stood at the window, staring out, still too bewildered to object.

Elton was rolling the dice over and over. Shaking them near his ear. Simon stayed seated, biting his lip and staring at the table hard enough to bore holes in it.

'Wait up.' Mia followed me down the stairs. 'That was a trick. Right?'

'I wish it was.' I reached the door and called back down the hallway. 'Thanks, Mrs Brett!'

'But . . .' Mia pursued me out into the cold and grabbed my arm to hold me back. 'Otherwise it's just crazy.'

I shook my head. 'From what I've been reading, the whole universe is built from crazy. Hopefully Demus will show up again and explain it all . . .'

'Demus? That's the guy?'

'Yeah . . .' I glanced up and down the street. No sign of Mother, or the Chrysler Avenger she'd been refusing to let die with dignity these past ten years. 'Listen. Could you . . . you know . . . get me more of that stuff? It really does help.'

Mia frowned, raising a hand to her bruised cheekbone. 'More? Are you feeding it to the dog?'

'I'll pay, of course.' I still had a fair bit left. Mostly, I had just wanted her to come round again. Now I'd gone and made it awkward. 'Never mind.' Though I did mind. The idea of being without the resin did feel a little frightening. I needed a barrier between me and my treacherous body right now.

'No.' She shook her head. 'It's not a problem. I'll hook you up.'

'Nick!' Mother beckoning me from the corner. 'Nick!'

'Gotta go.' I gave Mia an apologetic look.

'See you.'

And off I went, my mind full of her smile when any sane person would be too busy freaking out about bald stalkers with magic powers.

CHAPTER 7

'You've concluded that the many worlds interpretation, which, FYI, is correct by the way, is incompatible with time travel.'

Demus came from behind the bench and sat at the other end from me, room for a third person in between. Richmond Park lay before us, an early morning mist hiding the frost-laden grass, except where the ground rose in slight ridges, forming islands in a white and undulating sea. I hadn't come looking for him, but I had thought that he might find me. He was something of a magician after all.

He was right. I had concluded that. 'If every moment, an infinity of different worlds are branching from this one to accommodate all possibilities . . . then that's an infinite number of worlds from where time travellers could come back to this one. And since there aren't an infinity of time travellers arriving every moment, then either the many worlds interpretation of quantum mechanics is wrong . . . or time travel is impossible.'

I felt suddenly much sicker in Demus's presence, nausea pulsing in me. There seemed to be some sort of physical pressure, as if the space between us were overfull. Out of the corner of my eye I saw white shapes, phantoms like those I'd run through that night in the park. They were all around me, rising from the mist.

'Ignore those. They're just echoes. They'll die away,' Demus said. 'There's some sort of resonance between us, creating temporal anomalies, and it gets worse when we get closer. I've been waiting for it to wear off. My calculations suggested it would be much shorter lived. Think of it like a build-up of static electricity. I've been approaching you in stages, letting it leak away, rather than just walking straight up to you and letting the sparks fly.' He reached his bandaged right hand toward me and immediately the phantom images around us grew stronger, my nausea more intense. He drew his arm back, frowning.

'So all those weird déjà vu things that have been happening, all those ghosts in the park, all of it . . . that was all you? It all happened because you were close by?'

'Yes.'

'But why just for me? Why didn't anyone else see those things?'

'I think you might have already guessed that, Nick. You're taking this very calmly for someone who hasn't. But that's getting ahead of ourselves.'

'But—'

'Now, as I was saying, there are two reasons why we're not being crushed under a vast mass of time travellers right now.' Demus dug into his pocket. 'Biscuit?' He held out an orange flavour Club Bar. My favourite.

'No.'

He shrugged and started to unwrap it for himself rather clumsily.

'Hurt your hand?' I asked, impatience gritting my teeth together.

'Fractured a knucklebone punching that idiot.' Demus winced. 'Totally worth it.' He took a bite of biscuit. 'Anyway, as I was saying, there are two reasons why every past moment isn't besieged by time travellers. The first reason is a practical one. It's not the real reason but it's interesting. The thing is that it takes a vast amount of energy to travel through time; the sort of thing that requires a nation to put some effort in. And the theory is really complicated. I mean really. It will take you two decades to figure your way through it, and that's after I've sketched out the solution for you. But – and this is the important bit – it requires very little energy to create enough temporal micro-distortion to make that nation-sized effort fail. A small generator can make it impossible for thousands of square miles around it. And the theory behind the disruption is much easier. So, the cure is always discovered before the disease, and so if any government were worried that history might be rewritten by another government or that criminals might escape into the past . . . they build a few dozen disruptors as a precaution against new discoveries, and that's an end to it.'

'What the hell!' I pointed to the two phantoms running straight at us across the mist sea: Mia and me, terror on our faces. And behind us, sprinting with deadly intent, someone with a long blade . . . a machete! 'Is that . . . Rust? Ian Rust?'

The phantom Mia ran through us in a cold wash. Demus winced. 'It's an echo of a possible future.'

'Well, fuck that!' I raised my arms as the ghostly maniac ran at us and then broke into swirls.

'Pay attention.' Demus clicked his fingers. 'The second reason. The real reason that we're not deluged in time travellers is this: the arrival of the time traveller is an event like any other and branches a new timeline off from the reality he went back to. So, it's never crowded. And because his arrival creates a new branch he can do all those paradoxical things you hear about. He can kill his father as a little boy to prevent his own birth. He can meet himself. It won't matter, because he isn't affecting the timeline that leads to him, he is changing events on a new timeline.'

I nodded, still watching the mist nervously, then thought of the message I had scratched onto Simon's table. The one that had never reached me. 'So it's pretty useless to the traveller themselves, then. Because nothing they do has any bearing on the world they came from.

You could go back and kill Hitler, but it wouldn't save anyone you knew.'

'Bingo.' Demus put a finger to his nose and pointed at me with the other hand. 'There are altruistic arguments to say you might want to kill the bastard anyway, and give another possible world a better deal . . . but we don't care about that, do we?'

'I guess not . . .' In a universe where everything happened some-where, every good thing, every bad thing, it seemed pointless to care about anything but the world you were given. 'Is that—' Out on the field phantom Mia was wrapped in an embrace with . . . I couldn't say for sure. Now that I stared at them I wasn't even sure it was Mia. The figures were breaking apart, becoming hard to see. 'Was that—'

'So.' Demus waved the question away and leaned forward to stare at me. 'You know who I am?'

I did, though I felt silly saying it out loud. 'You're me. A me who survived leukaemia, but somehow never grew his hair back.' His face was proof enough. Now I saw it I couldn't un-see it. Two or three decades stood in the way, but we were twins. More than that, now I looked closely, I saw that he even had the faint, white seam of scar on his forehead where I had head-butted the coffee table at age two. 'You're a me . . . And, bizarrely, I'm as pissed off about the hair as I am pleased about the living . . . though common sense does say that one should throw the other in the shade.'

'I am.' Demus nodded. 'Technically it was *our* knucklebone I broke.' He leaned back and surveyed the park. 'It's more remark-able than just me being any old time traveller, though. I'm a you who remembers all this. A you that really shouldn't happen. I remember sitting where you are and having this conversation from your side. I remember me telling . . . me . . . about those dice rolls. You have to keep that piece of paper for the rest of your life, by the way. Or at least remember the numbers.'

I patted my pockets, suddenly terrified I'd lost it already. 'I can't—'

'It's under your pillow.' Demus grinned. 'So . . . I remember all this, and as long as I play my part, then what we do here really will impact my world. Our world.'

'Play your part?'

'I'm working to a script here, Nicky boy. I'm telling you what I remember me telling you. If I do something that I don't remember doing – say I threw you on the ground right now, or shot you – or even if I *don't* do something that I *do* remember doing – say I didn't explain this bit . . . Well, that could happen, there's nothing to stop it, but then we've branched away from my reality and I've lost my chance to make any difference.'

'If that happens . . . If you killed me, for example, then how do you explain your memories?'

Demus shrugged. 'Worst scenario would be that they'd be part of a genuine and dangerous paradox that could cause problems for the timeline as a whole. More hopefully they could be put down to madness, delusion, false memories created by a broken mind desperate for a solution to its woes. Even now, while we're still on track, all of those things are way more likely than an actual closed loop where I can come back and change my future. That should be impossible. But it seems to have happened. Maybe the right number of stars went supernova all at once and tied an impossible knot in space-time. Who knows? It should be impossible, but here I am, making my own memories.'

I tried to focus, but whatever this resonance he talked about was it was making it difficult to just stay upright and not vomit.

'OK, then why *are* you here? And can I have the cure for leukaemia that you must have brought back with you?'

'Sorry, Nick.' And to be fair, he did look sorry. Also pale and sweating, as if he was suffering, too. 'It turns out that unravelling the fundamentals of the universe is easier than stopping the human body self-destructing. Einstein had nailed the theory of special relativity and given us E=MC^2 on zero budget before people could listen to the radio, before the Wright brothers got a patent on their flying machine, and decades before antibiotics. By the time you're my age you'll have seen smart phones, the internet, and watched robots crawl over Mars, but we still won't have cured the common cold. Or cancer.' Demus finished his biscuit and wiped his mouth. 'It may sound creepy because I'm forty and she's fifteen . . . but I'm here for Mia, and I need you to get her to trust me.'

CHAPTER 8

Dizziness had swamped me and Demus had left before I collapsed. I'd started feeling better almost as soon as I lost sight of him.

It felt strange to know that the leukaemia wouldn't kill me. I should have been elated, jumping for joy, albeit like an old man. But instead I didn't feel anything really. Just burned out and empty. I still had to endure the treatment, the symptoms and the side effects. And as far as I understood things, if Demus's game didn't play out exactly the way he remembered it, then my survival would be up for debate again, too. The world would branch and I would no longer be the me who lived to become him.

The whole time travel claim seemed both ridiculous and, at the same time, the only possible explanation. And honestly, nothing had seemed quite real since Dr Parsons had sat me down to tell me that I had cancer two weeks earlier. A part of me had immediately started to expect a film crew to jump out from behind the curtains shouting, 'You're on *Candid Camera*,' and that part had been waiting ever since. Demus's appearance had only deepened my sense of the surreal and the hope that I might just wake up soon.

The thing about cancer, and I guess any disaster, is that it doesn't just go away. You don't wake up. And, in the end, you just have to get on with things exactly like everyone else does. Demus's appearance was the same, a strange fact I had to bend my life around.

Demus's parting words had been to get Mia to meet him in the park on Saturday evening. So now, in addition to having my own little voice inside my head telling me to call her and ask her out, I had . . . my own, older voice outside my head telling me pretty much the same thing. And I desperately wanted to ignore them both.

I wished Demus had told me more, but I guessed he could only tell me what he remembered telling me. He probably remembered my frustration, too. But somehow this loop of recollection and action had been frozen in place into Demus's memory, and if we broke it then all of Demus's certainty about what happened next would vanish along with whatever he was hoping to achieve. And since he was me, I assumed that his ambitions were in my best interest. At least he got to punch Michael Devis in the face. I could imagine how satisfying that felt, especially after twenty-five years waiting for it. I just wished Demus had shown up when Ian Rust did and kicked the shit out of him, too. Though, thinking about it, that guy was scary as hell whoever you were, and I guessed I was probably going to be no keener to meet him at forty than at fifteen.

Mia then. I lay on my bed staring at the ceiling, seeing her face. I could imagine doing it. Creeping to the telephone in the hall, dialling her number, easing the dial back after each digit so the noise of it resetting wouldn't bring Mother out as witness. 'Hi,' Mia would say. 'Hi,' I would say back, voice low, hopefully sounding seductive rather than like a boy scared his mother might come into the hall to ask what he was doing. 'Hi, Mia. Nick here. We should get together again. My place?' It seemed almost easy. I was admittedly slightly high on cannabis resin. The stuff had taken my pain and nausea and squeezed them into a corner where I still noticed them but wasn't tripping over them all the time.

I would, of course, need her number first. John had it, but he'd be full of questions. For all I knew, they were going out together already. Holding hands, snogging in the park . . . But then, if that were true, why had they come for me that night? Three's a crowd.

I could call John and he'd give Mia's number to me, but I would have to pay for it. Not in money. He had plenty of that. But in other less substantial currencies. And I wouldn't hear the end of it. 'Did she say no, Nick? Was she gentle with you? Did she laugh?' I didn't want John as an audience to this any more than I wanted Mother listening in the background. No, it had to be Elton.

Elton's comprehensive had the Wednesday off that week; Founder's Day, or something. I told Mother I was too sick for school, but not sick enough to stay in bed. She let me stay home and went to teach science to her current crop of students in the vague hope that, this year, at least one or two of them would make it into university. I'd never really understood why she had decided to teach. She wasn't what you'd call a people person any more than I was. I understood the choice of the sciences, though. It wasn't a subject traditionally sold through the warmth of the teacher's personality or their passion for the material.

She let me stay home with a defeated kind of air, where once she would have encouraged me to try to study and spoken of upcoming exams. Watching her leave and walk into the street it suddenly struck me quite how hard all of this must be for her. And, at the same time, I knew that Demus must have understood this thing for many years. Widowed by cancer, her only child struck down with another flavour of the same disease. It's always been hard for me to see myself through others' eyes, but I suppose that seeing Demus helped with that. Normally, just being fifteen wholly occupied my mind. The baby crawling toward the camera in the photo albums, the toddler with his bear and a red plastic car, that string of little Nicks linking this gangling teenager to the moment of my birth . . . none of that had shelf room in my thoughts. But Mother must see those children queued behind me every time she looked my way. And all of us were at risk.

I guess if either Mother or I had been a little less awkward in our skins, a little more Elton and a little less Simon, we would have been able to talk, to hug, to do the right thing and make all of this mess a little less terrible. But we weren't born like that, and couldn't.

I found myself hoping very much that Demus had found something useful to say to Mother that first night in the hospital corridor. From where he stood, she was of similar age. Perhaps in his future she was dead already, and he carried that around with him. My eyes misted and I realised that there was at least one thing about the future I didn't want to know. It would be enough to know that he'd found the words I couldn't and said something to help.

I took my bike from the shed and cycled to Elton's house. I may have wobbled a little and ignored the odd traffic light, but oddly cycling was less painful than walking, and a hell of a lot quicker.

Elton lived two miles away on the far side of Richmond Park. His flat was about halfway along the line that joined the gentrified heart of Richmond, with its stockbroker mansions and well-heeled townhouse terraces, to the concrete jungle of Brixton. During the Brixton riots last autumn – the second set of riots within four years in that area – you could see the smoke from Elton's window. A month later, they had another riot north of the river in Tottenham, and tried to stick a policeman's head on a pole. I'd asked Elton what he thought of it. He just shook his head. 'Nothing to do with me. That's Jamaicans, man. Is ten thousand miles from Jamaica to Madagascar.'

I'd considered saying the arguments behind the violence might have had more to do with the colour of people's skin rather than where that skin sailed to England from, but I didn't. The truth was I didn't know anything about it really. Not even what Elton and his family went through. And according to John it wasn't good. So, I shut my mouth.

When I pulled up, Elton was outside the block eating rice and chillies from a bowl. He always seemed to eat outside, unless it was raining. Cold, though, not a problem. He'd stroll back and forth along the strip of dying grass that ran between the flats and the low wall to the street. In the summer, other kids would lean out from their windows to chat. They all knew him. It seemed odd to me that Elton spent so much time learning to fight when he was the person least likely, out of anyone I knew, to have to. People just liked him.

The blocks were four storeys high, and sometimes when the little kids called to him, Elton would climb up the outside Spider-Man style to say hello. He had fingers like steel rods and zero fear of heights.

He saw me as I chained my bike to the gatepost and came across frowning. 'That won't last. Gotta bring it in.'

'Your place? Won't your mum mind?' The idea of cramming my bike into their tiny hallway worried me, muddy wheels on Mrs Arnot's linoleum. The woman was fiercely house proud, endlessly kind, and I lived in terror of her disapproval.

'She'll mind more if I have to chase down whoever takes it.' Elton nodded me toward their door. 'It's not locked.'

I took the bike in, leaning it against the radiator. The hallway was dim, the wall-space crowded with little knickknacks. The sort of comfortable clutter I always hankered after. Though Mother would never entertain that sort of thing on the empty magnolia acres of her walls. I breathed the place in. There was always something cooking, and it always smelled good. The TV burbled in the living room. Elton's brothers would probably be in there, maybe all four jammed on the sofa, watching a martial arts film on their Betamax.

Elton still had his frown when I came out again. He offered me his bowl.

'Hot?' I asked.

'A bit spicy.' I could see a light sheen of sweat on his brow despite the January chill.

'Best not.' I grinned. When Elton called something *spicy* it meant it would remove the skin from most other people's tongue. Everything smelled good at the Arnots' house, but you took your life in your hands if you put it in your mouth without a taste test first.

'I'm not happy with you,' Elton said.

'Me?' It was the last thing I was expecting to hear. 'What have I done?'

'Mia.' Elton narrowed his stare and took another spoon of rice.

'What?'

Elton ringed his left eye with finger and thumb.

I realised he meant the black eye Mia had at the last session. 'Me? You don't think—'

'I *know* you didn't hit her, moron.' He scraped up the last of the bowl's contents.

'What then? Who did hit her?' I'd been wanting to ask on Saturday, but never got the chance.

'I'm not happy with John, either,' Elton said.

'John didn't do that.' I couldn't believe it of him.

Elton waved the idea away. 'Both of you been getting her back with the wrong people. Dangerous people, Nick. A punch don't make no never mind. Those folk will cut you over nothing. Push them and you'll turn up on a missing person's list. These guys will wrap you in bin bags and sink you in the river. I ain't kidding.'

'But . . .' I raised my palms. 'I don't understand.'

'There's good places to get a bit of weed, Nick, and there's bad places. The people Mia knows are too far up the chain. Smart money pays a little more and buys off a local pothead, way down the chain.

Mia's dealing with Sacks, and getting store credit.' Elton shook his head as if this was madness of the worst sort. 'And don't say that name to anyone.'

'I . . . I didn't know.' I hadn't given it a moment's thought. I'd never heard of a 'Sacks'.

'Well, now you know.' Elton nodded. 'She's a nice person. Do her a favour and tell her you got another source. This ain't her thing, man. Girl's just trying to impress you.'

'Me?' I gave a hollow laugh and pulled off my hat. 'Really?'

Elton shrugged. 'I said she was nice, not clever.'

'I . . . uh.' I'd asked her to get me another slab of resin. 'I need her number then.'

Elton fished his little black book from the back pocket of his jeans. 'Phone boxes on the corner don't work. And you'll only get her crazy mother. Better to go over. She's in the Miller blocks, building three.' He took a pencil stub and wrote her number and address on a scrap of paper torn from his book. 'Go past the tube station, left past the Red Lion. You'll see the blocks from there.'

'Thanks.' I shoved the note in my pocket and blew into my hands to warm them.

'I'll watch your bike.' Elton started back toward his door. 'Better take it by tonight, though, or I'm selling the wheels.' He paused. 'Oh, and that trick with the dice. I'm going to need to understand that before next session. Can't have you rolling whatever number you want.'

I walked to Mia's place, limping by the time I got there. Whether my growing nausea was nerves or the chemo biting I couldn't tell. Either way it wasn't good.

The Miller blocks were four ugly towers, about fifteen storeys each. She lived on the eighth floor of the one furthest away. The plaza between the four sported two old sofas with their springs showing. Around the back of Mia's building was a burned-out car that had been there long enough to rust.

The lift stunk of urine and wasn't going anywhere. I took the stairs. They smelled slightly less and were still fit for purpose. Someone had sprayed their initials on the reinforced glass at every floor. The same person. I had to admire their egotism.

By the eighth floor I was winded and hurting. I hoped Mia liked her gentlemen callers pale and sweaty, because that was what she was getting.

Generally, I like to know what I'm going to say before I say it. I tried to picture Mia opening her door to me. Even in my imagination I stood there stuttering. I paused to catch my breath at the fire door from the stairwell to the main corridor. 'Hello' would be a good start.

The stairwell door sported a small rectangle of glass shot through with crisscrossed wires and badly fractured. It afforded me a partial view of the hallway beyond. I leaned in closer. A figure in a puffed-up black jacket was slouched against the wall about halfway down. It looked for all the world like Michael Devis.

CHAPTER 9

Fear is a strange thing. Along with its close friend, pain, fear is a vital part of the kit that evolution has furnished us with for keeping alive. Part of its effectiveness comes down to how hard it can be to overcome. If you have vertigo, then no amount of assurance that it won't hurt will get you to step off the highest board at the swimming pool. If you're scared of spiders, then 'it's a thousandth of your size' and 'they don't bite' are not going to make you pick one of the bastards up. Knowing that, in twenty-five years' time, I would punch Michael Devis in the face and enjoy it could not remove the fear of confronting him alone there in that dimly lit hall. And so I stayed where I was, dry-mouthed, heart pounding, and watched. What the hell was he doing here? He should be in school. A sore mouth wouldn't have got him off this long.

I waited a good ten minutes. It felt closer to an hour. Devis paced, kicked a can around, then scowled at an old man who opened his door until he thought better of complaining about the noise and drew back his grey head. Devis returned to can kicking for a while. Eventually, he went to the door at the centre of his pacing and pounded on it.

'I know you're in there! I'm not going away.' He strode off, turned sharply, and took to pounding again. 'I called him. I said I would. You want to be ready and waiting downstairs with me when he gets here.

He finds you're still hiding in your hole, and that shiner I gave you is going to seem like a love tap.'

I couldn't see the number on the door, but it was obviously Mia's. I had to step in. I had to do something. Instead I just stood there. Waiting. I tried to reach for the anger I knew should be inside me. Devis was the one who had hit her! And, at last, way later than my pride told me I should, I found the fury I needed in order to act.

The fire door squealed as it opened and somehow Devis heard it even above the racket he was making. He turned to stare down the corridor, not seeming to recognise me. I stood with my fists balled, wondering how badly he'd beat me before letting up. Rage and terror appeared to be two sides of the same coin for me.

In that moment, Mia's door opened and she stepped out, white-faced even without her Goth makeup. She had a rounders bat in one hand and swung it hard at the back of Devis's knee. He cried out, staggered, and began to turn while she landed a flurry of blows across his back. I started running toward them.

By the time I arrived, Devis had hold of the bat, at the cost of taking a nasty hit to his hand. I did my best impression of the flying kicks that Elton was always demonstrating and connected with his hip, sending him sprawling down the hall, the bat skittering away. I went down too, though a little less dramatically than Devis.

Both of them stared at me in astonishment. Devis from the floor, groaning and cursing. Mia from her doorway, wide-eyed. I got to my feet before Devis did and went to stand over him, panting with fury, fright, indignation, and all the other gifts a sudden surge in adrenaline gives us.

'Get the fuck out of here!' It wasn't the cleverest of lines. A hero issuing it at the D&D table would be mocked. But Devis seemed to take it seriously and scrambled past me, limping toward the stairs. He wouldn't have run from me on my own, but maybe Mia had really hurt him with her bat. Either that, or he was scared that Demus would show up to save me again.

He stopped at the fire door and looked back, mouth bleeding, the side of his face still bruised. 'He's coming. I told you that!' He looked frightened rather than pleased at the prospect.

I took a stamp-step toward him and he vanished, footsteps echoing down the concrete stairs.

'Christ.' Mia went to get her rounders bat.

'Uh.' I stood there feeling awkward, and no doubt looking awkward. The corridor smelled of old cooking. Baked beans perhaps.

'You should leave,' Mia said.

'I . . . uh.' I looked back down the hall. 'I'd rather come in. I had something I wanted to ask you.'

Mia still looked worried. She sighed and motioned with her head for me to follow.

'Keep your voice down. Mum's asleep.' She led through her front door, into the unlit hall behind, pausing to lean past me and put the chain on.

I followed, wondering how anyone who could sleep through Devis's hammering and shouting could be woken by mere conversation.

Mia took me into their living room. There was enough room for a sofa, armchair, and TV, with a small coffee table squeezed between, buried under copies of *TVTimes*. The room stunk of cigarettes, and their smoke stained the ceiling. Two empty quarter-bottles of whiskey lay on the floor by the chair.

'Sit?' Mia flopped bonelessly into the armchair.

'Thanks.' I sat on the corner of the sofa. The covers were stained, and I expected to find them sticky to the touch.

'You shouldn't have come.' Mia hunched in on herself, looking suddenly very thin. 'And you should definitely leave. You don't want to be here when he comes.'

'Who?' I tried to manufacture some confidence and sound reassuring. 'Sacks?'

She blinked at that. 'Sacks wouldn't come here. You get taken to Sacks.'

'Who then?'

'Some new psychopath on Sacks's crew. Young blood starting to cut himself a name.' She reached for a cigarette pack on the table and, finding it empty, crumpled it. 'He made a move on these blocks a few weeks back. Everyone expected Sacks to stamp him out, but he signed him up instead.'

'Stamp him out?' I snorted. 'It's not like this is Chicago. If people were being murdered left and right, it'd be in the papers!'

Mia raised an eyebrow at me, unsmiling. 'If a person goes missing, it's not a murder; it's a missing person. People run away from their lives every day. I think about it five times a week myself.'

'But—'

'They call him Sacks because if you cross him, he has you cut up, put into sacks, and hidden where you won't ever be found. You're not on the front pages as a murder victim. You're just another runaway.'

I swallowed and looked at the door. 'So, who's this new guy and what does he want?'

'He wants money. Or rather he wants to use the fact I owe Sacks to make me work for him.' She scowled. A fierce thing.

'Work?' I felt myself redden. 'What kind of—'

'That kind. The kind I won't do. The crew are always trying to get new girls. I guess this guy wants his own string.'

'Maybe the police . . .'

Mia's turn to snort. 'Should I start by telling them I owe money for drugs, or save that for later?'

'So, pay them. How much can it be?' I patted my pockets unconsciously. She'd got the resin for me, and then I'd asked her for more. This was my fault.

'It doesn't work like that.' Mia stayed hunched around herself. I wanted to take her hands, say it would be alright, do something useful, be the solution rather than the cause of the problem. 'Once you owe them, it's a loan. Loans have interest. The interest is whatever they say it is. It should have been a hundred quid. I gave that guy in the hall everything I could get together last week, eighty-six. He told me I owed two hundred.'

'Well, we find out how much they want, then pay it.' I had over three hundred in my building society account. I'd been saving since I was seven. And John could always loan us some. Money wasn't anything to him.

'How much do you think they'll add on for being hit with a bat?' Mia managed a half-smile.

'Go to the new guy. Forget Devis.'

'Devis?' Mia shot me a narrow look. Even with a black eye and no makeup she still looked achingly pretty. 'You know that creep?'

'Yeah . . .' It suddenly struck me how odd it was that I knew the thug hammering at Mia's door after a drug debt. And how crazy it was that, rather than some street hardened criminal, it was an only half-successful bully from a private school. A schoolboy. 'It's weird.' I stood, seized by an uneasy feeling. 'You didn't tell me what Sacks's new guy is called.'

Mia shuddered. 'They call him Rust. I don't want to know why.'

The knocking at the front door made us both jump.

We went into the hall, not hand-in-hand, but close enough together to know we both wanted that support. I could feel Mia trembling and my own hands shook. The knocking came again. A polite tap, tap, tap. Mia inched up to the spyhole and peered through. She pulled away as if bitten and motioned for me to look.

The fisheye view distorted Ian Rust's already weasel-like face into something from nightmare. A long, angular nose thrusting at the spyhole, his eyes dark beads to either side.

As if sensing us there he tapped again, and called out in a faux-sweet falsetto, 'Miiiiiiiaaaaaaaa! Oh, Miiiiiiaaaaaaaa!'

I jerked back and we both stood, paralysed, my heart pounding loud enough that Rust should have been able to hear it through the door.

'Miiiiiaaaaaa!' he crooned.

A pause, then movement at the letterbox. Instinctively, we both wedged ourselves to opposite sides. A glugging sound followed and a familiar astringent smell rose around us. White Spirit, perfect for cleaning paintbrushes, or for arson. 'Miiiiiaaaa!'

'Fuck!' Mia jumped back from the door.

'How do we get out?' I joined her and kept backing. We were on the eighth floor, and I doubted the flat had a back door.

'I have to let him in before he lights it,' Mia said. She raised her voice. 'Wait! I'm coming.'

Before Mia could move, a short, scrawny woman emerged from the opposite door in a nylon nightdress covered with cigarette burns. Her greying hair stood out in all directions and she had an empty whiskey bottle in one hand.

'Mum!' Mia made a grab at her, but the woman slipped by, swearing softly, and had the door open a moment later.

Rust seemed unfazed, his malicious grin not slipping a millimetre. 'So sorry to disturb—'

Mia's mother smashed the bottle on the doorframe and sliced the jagged stub across Rust's face. It took me by surprise, Rust less so. He jerked back with unnatural speed, but even so one of the glass points managed to cut him below the eye from his cheekbone to his nose.

'Bitch!' He stepped back, hand clasped to his face, blood leaking between his fingers.

'You want the rest?' Mia's mother followed him, raging, broken bottle held before her. 'Little bastard!'

Rust looked ready to spring, but the distant sound of sirens gave him pause. 'Mia.' He acknowledged her at the doorway. 'And I know you.' Fever-bright eyes found me. 'Nicholas Hayes. I know where you live.' His grin returned and, with his hand still pressed to his face, he hurried off to the stairwell.

Mia's mother shuffled back into the flat, ignoring both of us. She reeked of booze and seemed to have gone from raging to sleepwalking in moments. 'Clear that glass up.' Spoken to nobody in particular as she returned to her room.

'Shit.' Mia looked at me, looked at the fire door and the trail of blood drops leading to it, looked back to me. 'Shit.'

I opened my mouth, but could find nothing to add to her assessment.

'What are you doing here, anyway?' she asked.

'I . . . uh . . . I've got someone you need to meet.'

CHAPTER 10

'Where are we going?' Mia followed me, clutching a brightly patterned cloth bag at odds with her otherwise all black theme. She'd put on a jacket that was too thin for the season and she looked cold already.

'I told you. I know a man who knows everything.' I strode past the broken-down sofas, scanning the plaza for any sign of Devis or Rust. It seemed crazy that either of them should be here. I guessed that the drug dealing was Rust's extracurricular activity, and that now he'd been expelled he had decided to make it a career move. A 'normal' Maylert's graduate with a mind to try his hand at dealing narcotics would find a contact and sell on at a margin to their well-heeled friends, at public schools, at dinner parties, and the like. Rust, though, seemed possessed of the kind of crazy that wanted a more lucrative slice of the pie, joining the hard-core criminals at the source. And Devis, a born minion and too scared to say no, had been dragged in with him. 'Come on. Demus will know what to do.'

'You said he wanted to see me on Saturday evening.' Mia stopped to adjust her shoe.

'Yeah . . . Well, I figure he should know enough to know we need to see him now.'

'In Richmond Park?'

'Yeah.'

'That's miles away.' Mia caught me up.

'It's a fair way.' She had a point. We could collect my bike from Elton, but I couldn't exactly take passengers and it was a good walk, especially in a cold wind with the sun heading down.

'It's my best shot, OK?' I turned on her. We were in the street now, the four Miller blocks behind us. 'You want to stay here for Rust to come back?' I didn't much want to go home either. *I know where you live.* That's what he said. And nowhere feels safe with someone like Rust out there, biding their time. 'Seriously, this guy knows everything. He'll know we're coming early, and he'll know how to fix this. I can't explain better than that. Just trust me on this one.' I could explain better, only she'd think I was mad and wouldn't come.

Mia stopped again. I bit back a 'hurry up'. 'If he knows *everything*, and he knows we're coming three days early, then why doesn't he know to meet us here?'

'I . . .' She had a good point. 'That's a good point.' A very good point.

A black BMW with tinted windows rounded the corner from Station Road and roared toward us, squealing to a halt slantwise across the street.

'Shit!' I tensed to run. Rust didn't have a car. He was barely old enough to drive. Maybe turned eighteen. It had to be Sacks. He'd called in Sacks!

The driver window rolled down. 'Get in.'

It was Demus.

We didn't drive far, just a little past Elton's block. Demus parked in a side street.

'That's the guy!' Mia hissed at me the moment she got in. 'From the park.' Then, realising. '*This* is the guy you wanted me to meet?'

'Trust me,' I hissed back. 'He'll be able to help. He knows everything.'

Demus pulled up, turned off the engine, then turned to look at Mia over the back of the seat. For the longest time he didn't say anything, just stared. I have to admit it was more than a little creepy.

'What?' Mia demanded. She'd had a rough day and Demus got the sharp edge of it.

Instead of flinching he just smiled, a broad, happy, stupid grin.

'Think of a number, Mia,' I said. 'Any number you like. He'll guess it.' It's bad enough making a fool of yourself. Worse watching yourself make a fool of yourself.

Mia frowned. 'OK, diceman. I'm thinking of a number. What is it?'

'I don't know,' Demus said.

'What? How can you not know?' I pulled a stray D6 from my pocket. 'Call it. Show her!'

'That isn't going to work, Nick.' He shook his head.

'Why not?' My stomach lurched, the nausea returning after all the excitement. 'Have we gone off-script?' If he didn't remember this, then my recovery wasn't guaranteed anymore.

'No.' Demus said, not looking at me. 'I don't know what number you're thinking of, Mia, and I don't know what number that die would roll. But I know things about you. I know you don't have a favourite colour. I know you had a rabbit called Mr Woffles when you were six. I know your Aunt May died of a heroin overdose, even though you tell everyone it was a car crash.'

Mia reached for the door. 'Get me out of here, Nick. This pervert's been watching me. Going through my things.'

'I know about Robert Wilkins under the holly bush, Mia. You never told anyone that. You never told anyone how the old leaves spiked your bum, or that you saw a big orange centipede on the floor of that little cave in the holly tree and Robert tried to convince you it was magic. How could I know that? You never wrote it down.'

Mia was halfway out of the car, freezing air gusting in past her. She stopped. 'How are you doing this? Can you read my mind?'

Demus's voice changed. It went soft. 'I *know* because these are things you will tell me. I don't know the number you were thinking of just then because you never told me that.'

Mia moved back into her seat, pulling the door closed; still angry, but with curiosity winning out. 'What the fuck is going on?'

'I'm a time traveller, Mia.'

'Bollocks you are!'

'Mia, I know about the mud scraper outside your house in Barking when you were two. I know you have a crush on Siouxsie from Siouxsie and the Banshees and have sworn never to tell anyone. Either I'm a mind reader, or you're insane, or I came back from a time when you *had* told these things to someone. In fact, since we've just told them to young Nick here, you can assume I learned them from him.'

I sat silent, watching the exchange, wondering why Demus was hiding the fact that he was me. And how Mia couldn't see it anyway.

'But . . .' Mia frowned, unable to squeeze her objections into words. She slumped back. 'Tell me.'

Demus explained that when you come back through time you come back just as James Cameron predicted in Terminator. Buck naked.

'That was a lucky guess, mind. He just wanted to show off Arnie's muscles. The fact is, though, that it only works for living things. The equations that govern the universe don't care about time. There's no "now", no past or present, just a solution to the equation. That's how rocks see it. How atoms see it; planets, stars; antimatter, dark matter. None of it cares about "now". Time is just a variable. We make *now*. Consciousness makes now. We live it and we can, with sufficient energy, move it about.

'I took care choosing the place I came back to, as well as the time I came back to. I appeared outside the police station on Watkins Street at three in the morning of January the first. They assumed I was a drunken reveller and put me in a cell with some blankets. In the morning when they couldn't get any sense out of me, they rustled up some old clothes. Really nasty old clothes, it has to be said. And pushed me out the door.' Demus gave me a curious wink as if some kind of message were hidden among the detail. 'I went straight to the Ladbrokes on White Ladies Road. I've memorised the results of quite a few races and the race meetings on New Year's Day are always popular.'

'But you had no money, right?' Mia asked, hard-eyed and suspicious.

'I didn't. They wouldn't even let me stay in the shop. To be fair I did smell pretty bad. But just before the first three races that came up I called out the winner through the door. After the third time, several punters came out and asked my opinion about the winner of the next race. I told them on the understanding that I wanted a quarter of their winnings. After that I had money, then quite a bit of money, and lots of friends who didn't care how pungent I was.

'Next I had to find somewhere to live on a cash only basis and set up my laboratory.'

'Laboratory?' Mia asked. 'Figures that you'd be a mad scientist, I guess.' She slapped the seat. 'Shouldn't this be a DeLorean?'

'What?' I asked.

'A DeLorean, like the film.'

'Oh.' I knew she was talking about *Back to the Future*, but it only came out the month before, and I'd been kind of busy.

'Were you building something to get you back to when you came from?' I asked.

Demus shook his head. 'I was building two of these.' He reached over to the passenger seat and held up a circular device, a heavy-looking object like a metal headband sporting a collection of boxes and cylinders along its outer surface and connected to several cables. It looked rather homemade and significant amounts of duct tape had been used in its construction. 'I had to simulate the manufacture using current day materials before I came. It wasn't easy. But the technology I would have normally have used requires a massive infrastructure, and putting that in place would reshape the future. Which is exactly what I *don't* want to do.'

Mia slapped the seat. 'Wait!' She shook her head. 'I don't care about your gizmos. The important question, if any of this is real, is why the hell some guy from the fucking future is here, now, stalking Nick, talking to me in a car?'

It was true. That was the important question and I still had no idea of the answer, even though it was me doing it.

Demus stared at her, as if choosing his words carefully. 'I need to record your memories, Mia.'

Mia shot out of the car so fast I didn't have a moment to object even if I'd wanted to. She left the door open wide and sprinted off down an alley between two low blocks of council houses.

'Shit.' Demus put his space-age headband back down on the seat. 'Well, that went well . . .'

'Seriously, you knew to be there to pick us up . . . but you didn't see that coming?' Clearly I was destined to become stupid as I grew older.

Demus sighed. 'As well as recording memories, these devices can erase them. At some point in the near future you decide to erase your memories of recent events. *My* memories of them. By doing so you allow me to act however I choose without immediately jumping us off my timeline. I'm no longer forced to stick to the script. Things don't have to go how I remember things went . . . because I don't remember how they went. Events do, however, need to turn out the same as I remember them in the longer term.'

'And why did I choose to blank my memory back to some point between Mia getting into the car and jumping out of it?'

'You chose to do it that way because you remembered this conversation and realised that if you didn't blank our memories in just the way I described then you would not be me, your recovery from leukaemia would not be guaranteed, and my plans would be ruined . . .'

'If I buy that . . . and it's a big if, why didn't you remember that Mia needed money and just give her some? That would have avoided a lot of grief.'

'I shouldn't be able to remember any of this, if you recall. As soon as I showed up there should have been a whole new timeline. That's the way it works. As soon as there isn't a new timeline you start to drown in paradox, you set up an endless loop of second guessing yourself. Which is why it can't happen. But it did happen. Somehow that loop got frozen in place and we're stuck with what we got when the dial stopped spinning.' Demus lifted his hands helplessly. 'Over the next few days you are going to find yourself asking over and over "Why didn't he just do this instead?", "Why didn't he just go back to this time instead?", "It would have been so much easier if only . . ." And the answer to *every single one* of those questions is simply, yes, it would have been better, but that's not how I remembered it happening and so I didn't. Because if it doesn't go down the way I remember it, then we're on a new timeline, not mine anymore, and nothing I do here can make any difference to what happens in the future of my timeline after the point I left it to come back here.' He dug in the glove compartment and pulled out a thick wad of ten-pound notes. 'I knew she needed money. I can give her money *now*. I was going to do just that . . . but she's run off.'

After Demus's torrent of mind-bending nonsense, the money seemed like a cold, hard, actionable fact. Something I could use. 'Give it to me. I'll see if I can find her. She can't have gone far.' I reached for the offered cash and scooted along the back seat to leave by Mia's door.

'Bring her to the park on Sunday. Same bench!' Demus called after me. 'Tell her she's the one who sent me!'

He shouted more, but I was off and running.

CHAPTER 11

I headed back toward the Miller blocks and caught up with Mia on the way. I guess home exerts a pretty strong pull in times of trouble, even if it's the first place trouble will come looking for you.

'Wait up!'

'Go away!' She sounded angry.

'I've got money! Lots of it.' I limped ahead of her, spreading the notes out in my hands.

She stopped at that, shaking her head. 'This is crazy. Insane. That man . . . It can't be happening.'

'You sound like me when they told me I had cancer.'

'People get cancer every day, Nick. This is different.'

'*I* don't get cancer every day. It's different when it singles you out. Suddenly nothing makes sense. Just like with Demus.'

Mia sniffed and wiped at her nose. 'I know that. I'm sorry. I didn't mean . . .'

'It's OK. That's my problem. Not yours.' I held up a hand to deflect any objections and thrust the money at her with the other. 'Take it. I got you into this hole. This should get you out?'

Mia reached to take the cash, then stopped, her hand halfway between us. 'Taking credit got me into this mess. And they say to never borrow from or loan to friends.'

I smiled at 'friends'. I wanted to be her friend, perhaps more than was good for me. She made me feel like I was part of something, part of the world, not just skating around the edges, too tied up in myself to join in. 'It's not a loan. It's a gift. And it's not from a friend. It's from Demus, and I honestly don't know what he is yet.'

And it was true. I didn't really know who Demus was yet. I could be angry with last week's Nick Hayes. Just how far a person could grow apart from themselves in quarter of a century, I didn't know. Demus was wrapped around the same bones I was, and he had his memories of being me, filtered and edited by time and experience. But did that really make him me? Did we want the same things? Did we trust each other? Why on earth did he need to record Mia's memories anyway? That made no sense. I should have asked, but I'd been too eager to go after Mia before I lost her.

Mia took the money, glanced both ways down the street, and started to count it. It took a while. 'This could get me out from under Sacks. I'd have to take it to him. The other guy isn't going to take . . . seven ninety, eight hundred, eight ten.' She put one tenner in her pocket. 'Eight hundred.'

'No.' I remembered the glitter of Rust's eyes as he backed up the corridor, blood leaking between his fingers. 'You have to go to the police over that one. He's going to come after your mum.'

Mia shook her head. 'Any sign of the coppers and Sacks'd tell Rust to do what he liked. You don't grass. Not round here. Rust won't touch Mum. He'd be mad to.' She shoved the wad of money into her jacket pocket.

'Your mum knows karate, then?' I tried to imagine anything that would scare Rust off. Actually, a drunk with a broken bottle was scarier than karate, but I didn't think it would do the job.

'She knows how to look after herself.' Mia snorted. 'But that's not it. You don't know how come I can just go see a guy like Sacks.'

'I don't.'

'He used to be tight with my older brother. They came up through the gang together.'

'I didn't know you even had a—'

'Mike. He's in The Scrubs now.'

'Oh . . .' I considered asking.

'Wormwood Scrubs.'

'Prison?'

'Bingo.' She put a finger to her nose and pointed at me with the other. Demus's gesture. 'Five years. Drugs.' She shrugged. 'Anyway, Sacks knows my mum from when him and Mike were little. Loyalty doesn't run very deep with a guy like Sacks, but he likes to pretend it does, so he's not going to let a psycho like Rust cut Mum up. It would make him look bad. And he wouldn't have leaned on me so hard over the money. I mean, he would have held it over me, but he wouldn't have pushed *that* hard. Only, that message seemed to have been lost on the new guy.'

I blinked. 'So . . . is Sacks like, proper gangland, the firm, Kray twins and all that?' The Krays were ancient history and I had no idea what had replaced them, but I assumed something had. 'He's big time?'

'He wishes.' Mia laughed. 'He's on the edge of that, hoping to get a place at the table one day, but right now he just runs an area and pays his dues. If he put a foot too far out of line, there are real heavies who would come and shoot it off.'

'Unreal.' Somehow, Mia being two steps from the hard core of London's organised crime seemed every bit as difficult to take on board as Demus's visit did. I guess maybe because Demus at least promised a mathematical proof!

'Look, I'd better go,' Mia said.

'Uh . . . yeah.'

'I mean, I need to get this sorted as soon as. My head's a mess with all this craziness . . . and I have to see Sacks.'

'I could come. If you want me to. You shouldn't have to do this alone.' No part of me really wanted to go with her. I didn't want her to go either.

'Better you don't. Sacks doesn't take kindly to new faces.' She reached out to touch my arm. 'Thanks, though, Nick.'

She hurried off and I stood watching. One of the streetlights flickered into life as she passed underneath, glowing an uneasy amber-red. I could still feel her hand on me.

'Watch out for that guy,' she shouted over her shoulder as she turned the corner. 'He could be up to anything.'

I lifted my arm to wave and dropped it, feeling stupid. Slowly I turned for home, sick in my stomach and sore in every limb. I had chemo tomorrow. Another visit to the white world of stainless steel and starch, and the super-clean lie that everything would be alright. But I'd seen the future: one possible part of it had come back to see me. Know thyself. Philosophers have been urging us to do that since the ancient Greeks. I don't think anyone really does, though. But I thought I probably knew myself well enough to know that everything was far from alright with Demus.

I knew a few of the kids on the ward now. Eva was the only one who really talked, though. They say it's good to share, but in the end, whatever anyone says, we face the real shit alone. We die alone and on the way we shed our attachments. It started when I told the others I had leukaemia that day over D&D. Elton's hug had stayed with me. It spoke volumes about his warmth and goodness. But perhaps Simon's anger had been the most honest reaction there. He lacked the emotional wherewithal to translate it into something appropriate, but all of them were angry in their own way. I'd betrayed them. Broken the promise that I would always be there; that they could depend on me. Only Mia, who hardly knew me, was free of it. For her, it was part of her image of who I was now, not some ugly and unsettling addition. And, somehow, she hadn't run for the hills.

'What you thinking about?'

'Uh.' I looked up. Eva had come across, trailing her drip on a wheeled stand. She looked like shit, like she had been starved and beaten. Her hair had started to thin at last and her eyes had sunk into her skull.

'You're always thinking, Nick. Doing sums, thinking. Always inside. I'd get a headache.' She sat at the end of my bed. We were halfway down the ward now on our one-way, kill-or-cure trip. Make that kill or pause.

'I guess I am.' All of us have a shell, a skin between us and the world that we have to break each time we speak to it. Sometimes I wished mine were thinner. 'How are you doing, Eva?'

'Oh, good,' she said, and smiled a skull's smile. 'Apart from always being sick and everything. But the doctors say I'm doing well and I don't need to have that operation anymore. And I'm really glad about that. I mean really, really glad.'

I let her talk. It made her happy. I wasn't so sure it was a good thing she wasn't getting her operation. It sounded rather like they thought she was too far gone. But I hoped it was a good thing. I sat there and took my poison like a man. Or a scared boy. And tried not to let Eva be alone, or to be alone myself.

At visiting time Mother was first through the doors, looking tired and worried. It shocked me to see so much on her face, the severe lines that time and care had left there. I wanted to talk to her. Real things, not just lies about how I felt and shared promises about holidays we would never take when I got better. I wanted to talk to her like one person to another. But I couldn't do it. I didn't have the words. Maybe one day but not that day. And I realised that just as the disease was starting to take me away from the world, I was for the first time, in a short and self-absorbed kind of life, starting to really see it for what it was. The beauty and the silliness, and how one piece fitted with the next, and how we all dance around each other in a kind of terror, too petrified of stepping on each other's toes to understand that we are at least for a brief time getting to dance and should be enjoying the hell out of it.

Elton and Mia arrived about ten minutes later and shook me out of my strange state of mind. Of course, with Mother there they couldn't say too much, but Mia looked happier. She'd put on her war paint and cast herself in beautiful monochrome, all dark eyes and small smiles full of . . . something good.

We talked about nothing important. Somehow, I never questioned my assumption that this should stay between us and not be shared with Mother. I think I was protecting her from additional fear for her child, and less selflessly I was protecting my ownership of all this craziness that had dropped into my lap. I wanted to be the one making decisions about it . . . to the extent that decisions could be made.

Mia said something about putting her money in a sack, and I knew that the debt was settled. The details didn't worry me. I was just happy she was there. Pathetically happy, truth be told. Elton saw it, even if Mother and Mia mercifully didn't, and on their way out he shot me a grin that said so.

'Is that your girlfriend?' Eva dragged her stand over after her parents had left. She sounded in awe.

'Nah.' I leaned back on my pillows, unable to suppress a smile. 'But she is pretty cool, though.'

CHAPTER 12

I didn't make it to school again that week, but I made it to D&D at Simon's house that weekend. I took a bowl with me to be sick in, in case I couldn't reach the bathroom. Truth may often be the first casualty of war, but dignity is definitely the first casualty of disease. I was shiny headed beneath my black woollen hat now, and I looked as if I had stayed up all night for a week. I felt like crap, too. Demus must remember what it felt like to be this way; he'd lived through it and given me something to aim at. Still, I found it hard to forgive him for coming back from the future to make headbands that looked like props for a low budget sci-fi film, rather than to brew up some super cure; if not for the leukaemia, then at least for the nausea.

'That wasn't a trick.' Simon opened the door as I reached for the bell. 'The thing with the dice, it wasn't a trick.'

'How do you know?' I followed him up the stairs, taking my time.

'I thought about it. Hard.' When Simon said that, he meant he hadn't thought about anything else. 'I cut my dice open with a hacksaw. There's no way. Not unless you knew. And how could you know? You have some way of predicting the future? Then why aren't you a billionaire?'

I sat at the table and got my notes out, not answering.

'Well?'

'They're all going to ask the same question. Let me give my answer once.' I set down a rulebook with a thump that I hoped Simon would take for finality.

'OK.'

We sat in silence. John arrived and took his seat, joining our vigil, quietly getting ready. Elton and Mia arrived only five minutes later, though any five minutes that stretches a silence close to breaking point will feel like an hour.

Mia took her seat beside me, with a three-part smile: one third uncertainty, one third mistrust. And a last third that made me smile back and ran a warmth through me that seemed to drive back both sickness and pain.

'Spill it,' she said. 'They all want to know how you did the dice thing.'

'Right.' I looked around the table. 'First up, this is ridiculously hard to believe. I'm not asking you to believe it. I'm telling you what *I* believe. If you have a better theory, then I'll sign up to it because what I'm about to say really sounds as if the game has jumped off the table and taken over.' I shrugged. 'It is what it is.'

'And what is it?' John asked, serious, focused.

'The man who gave me the paper with the numbers on it. It's not just dice rolls he knows. He knows the winners of horse races. He knows things about me I never told anyone. He knows things about Mia *she* never told anyone.' I took a deep breath. 'Either he reads minds and predicts the future. Or he's *from* the future. He says it's the last one. He's a time traveller.'

'No way!' Elton leaned back, shaking his head, grinning. 'It was some dice trick. Dude's not from the year 2000. I'm telling you that. No how.'

'The future?' John kept staring at me. 'You know that's nonsense. Right?'

'Why does he know things about you and Mia?' Simon asked, frowning hard.

'You don't believe this crap, Si?' Elton's chair rocked back down onto four legs.

'It's the simplest explanation that makes sense,' Simon said. 'Even if all of you are in on it. Even if every one of you is lying to me . . . I did not let go of those dice after I rolled them. I took them apart. They were just solid blocks of plastic. There's no way I was made to roll those numbers.' He laid a new dice set on the table before him. 'The question is: how does he know these things about you two? Just being from the future doesn't do that.'

I nodded. 'I think you know the answer already, Si.'

'Because at some point between now and when he comes from, you must have both told him. Which means you probably trusted him.'

'Probably?' Mia asked.

'Well, he could have tortured the information out of you.' Simon rolled one of his new dice.

'I don't think he did that,' I said hurriedly.

'The question is, why would he come here, now, to us?' Elton said. He seemed to have reversed his opinion over the course of rocking on his chair. 'Because of your leukaemia, Nick? He brought you the cure?'

'Not that.' I tried not to sound pissed off about it. 'I think he *is* here to help, though. Because he knows us . . . Will know us . . . It's something to do with Mia. He wants her memories.'

'Well, that doesn't sound creepy. I think he's some sort of conman. Has to be. These guys are good at what they do.' John looked at Mia. 'What do you think about this?'

'And why,' Simon asked before Mia could reply, 'would he want me, John and Elton to know about him? There has to be a reason for the stunt with the dice. He didn't have to do that to convince you two.'

We kicked the idea and the question around the table until it all started to get repetitive. Slowly, we drew back from the notion that this was real and not a trick. Slowly, common sense began to stamp our collection of inconvenient facts into the ground.

'Time to play?' Elton asked at last, opening a coke.

'Hell yes,' John said. 'I've had enough of make-believe. Let's kill us some orcs!'

We started the game, and before long it had swallowed us as it usually did. The dice, the paper, and the figures relegated to the peripheries of a shared vision, the raw clay provided by Elton and shaped by collective effort.

We delved into caves beneath the ruined fortress that we had spent so long exploring and discovered a labyrinth that dwarfed the man-made one above. And in the deepest parts of those caverns, where black waters lapped on sunless shores, we found an abomination. Elton outdid himself setting the scene. He closed the curtains and read out his description of the thing haunting the depths into which we had unwisely ventured. The sickness made flesh, which had brought the fortress to despair and twisted the lives of those within it. A creature made of failures, of old cruelties, of stillborn children, missed chances, soured wounds. It spoke a language of pain, sewn from torture chamber screams and widows' weeping for lost lovers. And by the time John had skewered it through with his burning sword, the thing had struck down both my mage, Nicodemus, and Mia's priest. The creature's essence fled like a shriek echoing away in all directions, and even Simon's thief, Fineous, didn't ask after any tainted treasure it may have left behind.

'What's wrong with them?' John's warrior and Simon's thief had, with a hell of a lot of effort, got my mage and Mia's priest back to the surface.

'They're starting to fade from the world. Going grey, seeming faint. It spread from where the abomination touched them, but all of their body is affected now. The fingers and toes were the last to go.'

'I used my spell to cure the disease.' Mia pointed to her list.

'It can only slow it. This isn't a regular disease. There's magic at work.'

'I have a . . . divination spell . . . that means I can call on my god for guidance, right?'

Elton nodded. 'You call on The Man Jesus for his wisdom and cast your runes.' Elton wrote something and tore the paper into three pieces before handing them over. 'Three words: *Two. Sicker. Fort.* And a direction. Somewhere out there.' He indicated the great wilderness stretching out beyond the mountains in which the fort nestled. 'Out there among the dry stones.'

'And how big is this wilderness?' John asked.

'You've only got rumours to go on, but it's big.' Elton spread his hands. 'Biblical, brother. Forty days and forty nights shit.'

'Locusts and honey,' I said.

'You wish!' Elton shaded in a whole lot of nothing on the map. 'You go out there, and before long you're going to be begging to eat a nice juicy locust.'

We spent the rest of the session wandering in the wilderness. It sounds dull, but sometimes focusing on the simple but necessary mechanics of life on the hard edge can be quite therapeutic. In place of orc hordes, vampires, and abominations, our enemies became hunger, thirst, and exposure. We concerned ourselves with food, water, and shelter, and for a city boy Elton seemed to know a lot about just how difficult those things are to acquire in a trackless waste.

'Your ride's here, Nick!' Simon's mum, yelling up the stairs with her usual gusto.

I swept my stuff into my bag, dodging questions about whether I'd make school in the week.

'How you doing, Nick?' Elton blocked my way as I tried to leave.

'I'm fine.' My eyes prickled. I've never been good at having people care about me.

He grinned and shook his head. 'You'd say that if your leg had just fallen off. You ain't fine, man. You're in the shit and we all know it. But we're gonna pull you out. You even got some crazy guy says he's from the future to help. Probably put his robots on the case. But you ain't fine, so don't say it.'

'OK.' I struggled to keep my voice steady. 'I'm not fine. I feel like I'm dying . . . Also, some bastard's given my D&D character fading sickness.'

'Better.' He punched me on the shoulder and stepped aside. 'Henri is twenty-one on Thursday. Party, Friday night. You're coming. John and Simon, too. No excuses.'

'Yes!' John punched the air. Parties at the Arnots' were a thing of legend, and Henri, Elton's oldest and coolest brother, was enrolled at dance college where he was literally the only male student in his class. Which meant his guest list would be packed with female dancers.

'I can't.' Simon shook his head.

'Can and will,' Elton replied firmly.

I glanced at Mia. She nodded, which I took to mean she was going. 'See you tomorrow.' She hadn't forgotten our 'date' in the park. Me, myself, and Mia: our very curious trio.

John raised his eyebrows at Mia's 'tomorrow' and I offered him a grin before lifting a hand in farewell and setting off down the stairs. 'Later.'

Another week to our next session, another five days to the last chemo cycle of my first course, another six days to Henri's party. My own wilderness stretching ahead of me. It might only be a week, but something told me that forty days and forty nights might not be enough to cross it.

CHAPTER 13

'Hey.'

'Hi.' Mia was waiting for me at the gate we used on 'vampire night'. Richmond Park stretched out behind green-painted iron railings, an uninspiring expanse of wet grass.

Mia shrugged away from the gatepost and came to walk with me, breath fogging the air. A light, annoying rain had started up, the super-fine kind that gets in your eyes and coats your face.

'So.' Mia kept close to my side. 'This is kind of crazy.'

'Very.' I liked having her close. 'I'm glad you decided to come.'

'It's not really the sort of thing you can just walk away from,' she said.

'No.' I knew that Demus had helped her out with the money, but if she was like me then the real reason she was here was that, after the initial shock of it had sent her running from the car, the mystery of it niggled at her. And an itch like that has to be scratched. 'I want to hear what he says.'

'If it's true . . . what he says . . .'

'It makes you wonder what you can be sure of anymore. If anything is certain. What really matters.'

'Yes.' Mia stopped and looked up at me. 'Exactly. All those things.'

'I'm good with questions. Answers . . .' I shrugged. 'No sign of Rust since . . . ?'

'No.'

We started walking again. Nobody I knew had seen Rust since he got cut. It made me uneasy. Like a shark's fin vanishing beneath the waves.

'So, do you think Simon will come to the party?' Mia asked.

'No.' I didn't think I would either. The thought of a party both thrilled and appalled me.

'Why?'

'I can think of about a thousand reasons!' The Arnots' parties were a thing of legend and this would be my first chance to experience one for myself. But I was hardly at my best.

'Name one.'

Rather than choose one of Simon's many reasons, I decided to offer up my own worst fear. 'Dancing, for a start.'

'Dancing?' Mia laughed. 'It's not like you're expected to do the waltz and the foxtrot, or do it in squares like a barn dance. It's just . . . you know . . . dancing! Like on *Top of the Pops*, but with less lamé and glitter.'

'He won't do it. He can't.' *Top of the Pops* was another of my mother's guilty TV pleasures, and I'd been watching the audience bounce around to the top twenty for years. But I still had no idea how it worked, and no desire to demonstrate that fact in front of Mia, with a backdrop of Henri's dance school hotties showing everyone how to really do it.

'Nonsense. Get over to Simon's during the week and make him have a go. It's as easy as climbing stairs. Move around a bit in time to the beat and that's all there is to it. You don't have to do anything fancy.'

'Yeah. I . . . uh. I'll tell him.'

'Don't tell him. Go there. Make him have a go, then make him come. Seriously.' Her hand brushed mine. It could have been an accident. 'It would be stupid if he didn't go.'

Demus was waiting on the bench, wrapped in a heavy coat. Black, unmoving, and ominous.

'He *is* like that vampire,' Mia muttered as we approached.

'Sorry?'

'In the game,' she said. 'Sucking away memories.'

She had a point. In D&D a vampire's touch robbed you of experience. It took away what you'd learned and left you as a shadow of what you were. I didn't like to think of myself in those terms. I hoped Demus had an explanation that showed myself to me in a better light than that. So far, as a mirror he had proved to be very troubling.

Demus glanced up when we drew near, my own worries echoed on his brow. He looked tired and the rain beaded on his baldness.

Mia sat at the far end of the bench. I sat between them.

'How do you know me?' Mia's first question.

Demus leaned forward to look at her across me. 'I'm no expert, but I'm pretty sure it isn't good for anyone to know too much about their future. So, let's forget the how, and leave it at the fact that I do know you and I want to help.'

'OK . . . Why do you want to take my memories?' Mia wasn't wasting time. John had wanted to know if they had hover-boards in the future and what Mars was like. Mia, sensibly, was all about Mia.

'Good question. I don't want to actually take your memories. I just want to copy them. But the "why" is still valid.' Demus rested his elbows on his knees, chin in hands. 'Years from now, you have a very serious accident. You have a brain injury. The injury is repaired using stem cells, but that's like rebuilding the library, putting the shelves back up, and putting new books on the shelves . . . Only, all those books are blank.'

Mia managed to look horrified and sceptical at the same time. 'What kind of—'

'It doesn't matter. What matters is that you're now old enough that the architecture of your brain is fixed in place. A record of your memories now, along with updates made every five or ten years until the accident, would allow those memories to be reinstated into your repaired brain, restoring everything you've lost.'

'Why . . .' Mia frowned furiously. 'Why . . . don't you just tell me what the accident is, and then I can avoid it?'

'Ah. Well. There it becomes complicated. Nick's already told you about how quantum mechanics reveals to us that every action splits the universe into a great many new versions where each possible result plays out. The simplest answer to your question is that in my timeline I didn't tell you what the accident was. So if I were to tell you now, then we wouldn't be in my timeline anymore. And if we're not in my timeline then the accident may not even happen, or my advice on avoiding it might *make* it happen. And yes, one of the multiverse's infinity of Mias may avoid that particular harm, but the Mia I know, the one that's *my* friend, will still be a helpless shell of what she was, and my efforts to restore her will have failed. I can't change my past. I can't change that part of your future that is already in my past. But I *can* change my future, and you are in it.'

'I think my head's going to explode,' Mia said.

'Well . . . if it did, it would save an awful lot of bother.' Demus leaned back.

'Why do you have two headbands?' The question had been puzzling me all night.

Demus dug in his pocket and brought out a plastic rectangle large enough to cover his palm.

'What is it?' Mia reached across me to take it and he let her.

'Cutting edge technology.' Demus snorted.

'I know this! Simon has one in his collection.' Simon didn't have a computer. Well, he had a ZX Spectrum. But he spent a lot of time on the ones at the university where his dad worked, and had a stash of manuals about main frames, the serious sort of computer that they used in academia and industry. He also had an assorted collection of related bits and pieces that his dad brought home. 'It's a new type of floppy disk.' It was smaller than the ones for my Commodore and encased in plastic.

'Not so floppy now.' Mia grinned and stroked it.

'It holds about a megabyte of information,' Demus said. 'We need to store terabytes. It would require *millions* of these. A big truckload. And writing to them would take decades. You just don't have the technology required to record memories.'

'Well, you're screwed then,' I said.

'No. That's why I made two headbands.' Demus stood and began to pace. He had a noticeable limp. 'I need to record Mia's memories in your brain, Nick.'

'No fucking way!' Mia jumped to her feet.

'They'll be encoded. He won't be able to access them.' Demus raised both hands. 'Secrets safe.'

I shook my head. 'Don't I . . . need the space they'll take?'

'You'll be fine.' Demus waved the objection away. 'Just follow the instructions every five years. It takes an hour or two. And decades from now, it can all be downloaded into Mia's brain, and she gets her life back. Easy.'

Something about his frown told me it wasn't going to be that easy.

'But . . .' I invited.

'But the headbands won't work yet,' Demus said. He limped away, turned round, limped back. 'The electronics I need can't be bought yet.'

The wind picked up and the rain turned from a mist to a steady patter. The chill cut through my coat and found my bones. I sat on the wet bench looking out over the wet fields at distant housing, a dripping forest behind me. Suddenly I was as miserable as I had ever been.

'You couldn't have found this out before you came back?' Mia asked.

'I could, and did. But the timing wasn't mine to choose.' Demus slumped back on the bench, beside me. He set a hand to my shoulder. 'Chin up, kid.' Perhaps my current low moment had punctuated his memories deeply enough that he still remembered it. 'I need a better microchip than the ones on offer. A 32-bit processor at a minimum. A Motorola 68030 will serve. Just. But I can't buy one. They do exist, however. Two years from now I'll be able to order one.'

'So why not just come back to when they *can* be bought?' Mia persisted.

'The answer to pretty much every why-question you have, all of which are perfectly reasonable, is simply this: I remember coming back to 1986. I remember that I didn't show up in 1988 when all of this would have been much easier. When whatever tied a knot in our time-line happened, this is where the pieces fell. If I change anything, and I can, then it will no longer be the timeline I remember, and nothing I do can help the Mia I left behind.' Demus sighed. 'And the net result is that I need this chip, and currently the only examples of it are the prototypes held in research labs at several locations across the globe.'

'Right, so you're going to go all James Bond and steal the micro-chip from a high-security Tokyo laboratory?' I laughed out loud. It was almost less feasible than time travel.

'No. But now I get to answer the question you forgot to ask. The one about why I roped your friends into this. First, though, let me ask you a question of my own.' Demus wiped the rain from his scalp. 'What is it that John's father does, exactly? You know. To make all that money?'

CHAPTER 14

'John?'

'Yes?' He sounded odd, but it was a bad line, full of crackles and fizz.

'Emergency!'

'What?'

'None of us know how to dance.'

'You mean you and Simon don't.'

'When have *you* ever danced?'

'At my cousin's wedding last year. There was a disco at the reception. I'll have you know that I've got moves.'

'We're coming over.'

'When?'

'As soon as I've tricked Simon into coming.'

A long silence filled with crackles and the ghosts of someone else's conversation, then, 'OK. At least it'll be funny.'

I hung up and leaned against the counter. 'It's on.'

Simon's phone was in the kitchen. It seemed wrong somehow. In my experience phones were in the hall, private things. But Simon's mother apparently had no secrets, nothing to say on the phone that couldn't be said within two yards of the kitchen table. Which was where both she and Simon's little sister, Sian, sat watching me expectantly.

Their cat, Baggage, had wound herself around my ankles and lay there shaken by loud purrs, as if she had realised some long-held ambition.

'What are you going to tell him?' Sian asked. 'He won't go there without a good reason. I mean a reason he thinks is good.'

'I'll tell him we need to do some planning for our next D&D session, and that John can't come here because . . . he . . . he's grounded until Friday.'

'Nice.' Simon's mum nodded. Ever since the idea of getting Simon to a party had been mooted she'd been wholly on board. 'I'll give you a lift over there as soon as he gets home from school. I've always wanted to see this alleged mansion of John's.'

Half an hour later we pulled up in John's gravelled drive. We were buzzed through the automatic gates at the street, and the house had remained hidden behind leylandii trees until the sweep of the approach revealed it.

'Fuck me sideways!'

'Mum!' Simon's protest went unheeded.

'It's like a stately home. In Richmond.' Simon's mum gawped without shame. 'Go on then. And Simon, if there's even the *slightest* chance he's gay, make sure you marry him!'

Simon shot out of the car faster than anyone of his girth should have been able to. I suspect most teenage boys could win the hundred metres in an attempt to outdistance parental embarrassment. I followed quickly, calling back my thanks for the lift.

I joined Simon on the steps beneath a porch supported on grand columns. The doorbell was an ivory disc at the centre of a ridged brass plate and the chime it caused sounded both deep and distant.

I always expected a butler to open John's front door. A tall, immaculately tailored man with a pencil moustache straight out of the 1930s.

John in a T-shirt, jeans, and socks was always something of a let-down. This time, though, it was Mia, barefoot, in a man's shirt and black leggings, and the sight of her did something complicated to my insides.

'Come on.' She walked off down the broad, tiled hallway. The distant strains of a piano reached us.

We took our shoes off and hurried after her. We all had the afternoon off due to a frozen pitch cancelling games and I'd taken the morning off, too, so I could scheme with Simon's mum. What Mia's excuse for being here before four on a Wednesday was, I didn't ask. John was in one of the living rooms, playing on their grand piano. He was sickeningly good at it, and the piece was unashamedly romantic.

'Such a show-off!' I came to stand next to him, watching his hands flow across the keys.

'Jealously is an ugly thing, my boy.' John finished with a flourish. 'Simon! You came! I didn't think you would.'

Simon put his bag on the polished mahogany expanse of the piano. 'Why not? I don't want to die in this wasteland any more than you do.'

'Ah.' John grinned at me. 'You told him this was about D&D. Cunning.'

'You're here to dance, Simon.' Mia reached for his hand.

'You lied!' Simon pulled back, scowling in my direction. 'I'm going.'

'You can't. Not unless you want to walk the whole way.' I claimed his bag from the piano. 'Also, I have important news from Demus to discuss . . . after.'

John played a 'Dun! Dun! Dun . . . !' on the deep notes, then got up and walked across the room. 'You're here for the same reason Nick is. You're going to your first Arnot party and you're both afraid of dancing. And girls.' He reached the hi-fi system, a monster of a thing that managed to convey the sense that it was both horribly expensive and at the same time very, very cool. A work of finest German engineering capable of delivering Motown's hottest beats with clinical efficiency. 'Fortunately, I have gathered together examples of both. Music . . .'

He hit the play button and the opening bars of 'Wanna Be Startin' Somethin'' filled the room, Michael Jackson joining in quickly enough with his curious mixture of ooos and ahhhs, as if he were easing into a cold bath. 'And the lovely Mia is here to represent the female half of the species.'

Mia made a mock curtsey.

We stood, looking at each other. Mr Jackson was doing his level best, but the degree of awkwardness with the four of us in a brightly lit room was sufficiently high that, with a gun to my head and the option to dance or die, I would have happily opted for the sweet mercy of a bullet.

'Wait.' John was starting to look as uncomfortable as I felt. He ran for the lights and dialled down the dimmer to squint level. 'This is a lot easier with a beer in you. Trust me.'

Mia approached Simon and began to swing her hips. Michael Jackson was beginning to start something at last. 'It's easy,' she said, reaching for his hands. 'You can't do it wrong, except by just standing there.'

And somehow, she made it happen. It wasn't down to her enthusiasm or cajoling, it wasn't even the pretence of anonymity in the half-light, or the implicit vow of silence, a secret pact never to be spoken of. It was just something in her. Kindness maybe. But in the space of a few minutes all of us were dancing, badly, and just not caring. And John, for all his money, looks, and mastery of the piano was, by far, the worst of us!

We danced through 'Startin Somethin'' into 'Baby Be Mine', where I watched Mia, and on into 'The Girl Is Mine', where John and I exchanged speculative glances.

I had come to the house hurting and sick, dreading the whole thing, even as I played along that it was Simon who needed the lesson, not me. A large part of me had zero interest in going to a party. That part wanted to curl up around my illness, to turn in on itself and wait to be reprieved or to die. Even a good chunk of the part of me that said I should go was saying so out of a sense of guilt. The guilt that people on a timer feel about wasted opportunity. The big C had wrapped itself around me, and here I was thinking of letting my first real party slide by because I felt sick and I might make a fool of myself on the dance floor?

But when the beat took hold and I let myself go, it seemed that the pain and even the nausea took a back seat, replaced by a joy that was, in part, relief, but mostly just the simple primal pleasure of the dance. And yes, it was also true that some fraction of it was also down to the fact that although John Featherstonhaugh might have music at his fingertips, when it came to Motown, the rest of him jerked around with about as much sense of rhythm as an epileptic cow. It was true when he had joked that jealousy was an ugly thing. And true that I was jealous. Mia felt increasingly precious to me, even though so little had passed between us. To John, I knew she would simply be a conquest. Not treated badly. But not . . . valued to her true worth.

Inevitably 'Thriller' arrived, after which the needle parted company with the vinyl and we stood just a touch out of breath, a touch sweaty, starting to feel the embarrassment rise around us once more.

'You see,' Mia said, laughing. 'Easy. And you're all coming to the party, or I stop coming to D&D.'

'OK.' Simon agreed without hesitation. I think it was the D&D threat that did it. Mia was part of our group now. And those ties run deep. You don't abandon a party member. Even if it means going to a party.

'So what did Demus say?' John asked.

We had adjourned to another living room and were distributed along the length of two huge leather sofas, the over-stuffed kind punctuated with deep-set buttons; Mia and I in one, facing Simon and John in the other.

'Well, for starters he told us what your dad does,' Mia said.

'What does his dad do?' Simon asked.

'John's father is, among other things, the chief financial officer for Motorola UK,' I said. 'He is also on the board of directors and a significant shareholder in the parent company.'

'This is news?' John stretched. 'I've told you this before.'

'Yeah . . .' I deflated somewhat. 'Well. I wasn't listening.'

'So why does he care what my father does?'

'To make the gadget that's going to record Mia's memories, so she can be healed after her accident—'

'Wait! What?' John raised his hand. 'Accident?'

'He didn't say much about it, but she gets hurt and we need to record her memories to put them back afterwards.'

'This sounds like bullshit.' John pressed his lips into a thin line.

'His gizmo won't work without a 68030,' I said.

'I have no idea what you're talking about,' John said.

'It's a microchip.' Simon shuffled along the sofa. 'In development. Not yet released.'

I would have asked how Simon knew this shit, but it was the sort of stuff that he always knew. Anything from the gauge of an unknown stretch of rail track in the Alabama mountains to the specifications of an unreleased microchip.

'Well then, he waits until it comes out and buys one,' John suggested.

'Not an option, apparently.' I tried to sound apologetic. After all, technically it was me that was causing all this trouble. Or would be. 'It's all got to happen before the end of next week.'

'So . . .' John spread his hands.

'So that's why he proved himself to you guys,' I said. 'With the "batter up", and knowing all the dice rolls.' I took a deep breath. 'He wants us to steal one for him.'

CHAPTER 15

'Industrial espionage? That's what this is all about?' John punched a cushion. 'I knew this was all nonsense. The guy just wants to steal a march for one of the competitors. You know how much the research behind a new chip is worth, right? *Hundreds* of *millions*!' He punched the cushion again. 'I knew it.'

'He's from the future,' I argued. 'This new chip is like a steam engine to him. He doesn't want to steal the ideas. Just the thing.'

'With stakes this high he could afford any amount of special effects to fool us into believing his story.' John started to pace around the room. 'Think about it. He just happens to need this fabulously valuable thing to save our friend. In the future. It's not like Mia's in any danger. She doesn't need saving.'

'What I don't understand,' said Simon, unswayed by John's passion, 'is why he thinks we'll be able to steal this chip for him. Even if you could argue that John might be helpful, that still leaves me and Elton. We're not exactly top of the cat burglar list. He'd be better off kidnapping John and mailing pieces of him to his dad until he hands over the chip.'

'Thanks.' John favoured Simon with a rather ungrateful stare.

'He needs John because just before Christmas John's father took him on a bring-your-son-to-work day to the laboratory where the

Japanese have sent a prototype of the chip for testing. John knows where it is and the rough layout. He needs *you* because he thinks you can hack into their mainframe, like in that film *WarGames*. I told him you couldn't, but he says you can. He thinks you can find the combination for the safe where the chip is stored overnight. And he needs Elton because the easiest way of getting in is through the roof, and since Elton is practically Bruce Lee, he's going to be able to scale security fences, climb buildings, and suchlike. You've seen what he can do.'

'If he's got money, can't he just hire people to do this for him?' Simon asked.

'It's a question of contacts, timing, and trust. He doesn't know who to ask. He doesn't have time to find out. And if he did, he couldn't trust them.' The real answer was that he remembered that they were involved. Not a direct memory, because apparently I was going to wipe those, but from information he gathered later. And if he remembered they were there, then they needed to be there, or none of this would work for him . . . and me. I felt selfish asking, but twenty-five years of guaranteed life, and more on offer, looked pretty damn good from where I sat, so I needed Demus to be my future. I needed my Mia to be his Mia.

'Why does he think Simon could get information out of the main-frame? Or even get on it in the first place?' John asked.

'He says you'll be able to find or guess your father's password. He says it's probably written down somewhere. Most likely inside his wallet. And he knows that Simon has been breaking into protected files on the mainframes at his dad's university for years.'

They both looked at Simon, who coloured and stared at his hands. 'There's no law against it.'

'See!' I said. 'Demus says the security in computers during the 80s is a joke, and that anyone with a good understanding of the operating system should be able to root out the combinations for the lab safes.'

'If they're recorded on the system,' said Simon.

'He seems sure they are,' I said.

'So, all he wants us to do is rob my father's work of their flagship new product, then?'

'Yes.' I hadn't really expected John to leap at the opportunity. 'They won't really be losing anything, and it will help save Mia.'

'Who doesn't appear to need saving from anything,' John said.

I fell back into the sofa. We had all been standing practically face-to-face, close to yelling. I let exhaustion take me. 'I believe him.' I could have told them what Mia's eyes had failed to tell her. I could have said that Demus was a future me, and if we kept to his script, if we allowed our timeline to be his, then my recovery was a done deal. I could have but I didn't. It was too close to begging and something in me wouldn't allow it. 'I believe him and I'm going to try to get this chip with or without you lot. But I won't succeed without you.'

'Then why try?' Simon asked.

'Because you guys would try on my behalf if you believed it. And Mia's one of us.'

A tapping at the window stopped John from having to answer. Elton bounced into view, jumping to be seen.

'I'll go let him in.' John set off on the long trek to the front door.

'Why didn't he just ring the bell?' Mia asked as John left the room.

'John's mother doesn't like him in the house.' I looked at the floor.

'Why not?' Mia paused. 'Elton's the nicest guy ever. He's always polite. He calls my mum "ma'am".'

'Wrong colour.' Simon had less of a problem saying it than I did. He never really understood how people treated each other anyway.

'Jesus!' Mia flopped into the sofa beside me. 'Fuck.'

'Fuck indeed,' I said. 'You can't choose your parents, but John's mother is always a reminder to me that I got a pretty good deal.'

We sat in silence after that, until John came back, Elton on his heels.

'Hey all.' Elton perched on the arm of the larger sofa. 'Who died?' He looked edgy. Nervous. Not like Elton.

'It's nothing. We're still in shock from seeing John's dancing.' I made a smile. 'Also, you missed the bit where I told them that Demus wants us to rob a computer lab.'

'I ain't breaking in anywhere.' Elton shook his head. 'No way. Mum would kill me. And then my brothers would stamp on my corpse.'

'He says it's to stop Mia from being a vegetable after the accident she has when he comes from,' John said.

'Man, these fairy stories again? Breaking and entering because of some trick with the dice? Ain't happening. I mean like *no way*.'

The argument that would have followed was stopped in its tracks by another tap on the window.

'Fuck! That's the guy!' John stared with the rest of us at Demus. I was as surprised as the rest of them. He'd said nothing about showing up.

For a moment all of us stood staring. All of us except Simon, who glanced from Demus to me and back again. Simon looked at the world differently. He was the sort to notice the number plate of the car hurtling toward him. The rest of us would be busy getting out of the way.

'What's he want?' Elton asked.

'We could let him in and find out,' I suggested.

And a minute later Demus was among us, standing there in one of John's living rooms in his trench coat, a solid and inescapable fact. Still, only Simon seemed to have seen past baldness and a quarter of a century to notice how alike Demus and I looked.

'Turn the TV on.' Demus took us all by surprise.

'Why?' John asked, but he did it anyway. The big colour TV flickered into life, one of about four in the house and twice the size of any I'd seen anywhere else.

'BBC 2,' Demus said. 'Quick as you like.'

John punched the second channel button. The screen showed crowds of people standing in bright sunshine . . . some kind of sporting event. It looked chilly; they were well wrapped.

'What's the time?' Demus asked.

'You're wearing a watch.' Simon pointed to it.

'Humour me.'

'Four thirty-six.' Elton read from his digital watch.

'Half past.' Mia pointed to the wall clock.

The footage panned across the crowd to the space shuttle, engines fuming gently on the launch pad. The announcer reminded us that we were watching live at T minus one minute.

'It's going to explode seventy-three seconds into its flight,' Demus said. 'I'm sorry to use the deaths of seven people in this way, but it's important that you believe me. It's also important that you understand that for me this has already happened. I can't change it.'

'T minus thirty seconds.' The official countdown from the NASA control tower now.

'You could be beaming this in,' muttered Elton.

'It will be in the evening papers, with the time.' Demus went to turn the volume up.

We watched as the engines ignited and the shuttle shuddered on its powerful rockets, slowly ascending on a pillar of fire. I didn't want it to explode.

The shot switched to images of Americans craning their necks as the shuttle took to the skies. Smiles and awe, flags waving, an image of the families and senior officials. Beside me Demus's silent count became a voiced one. 'Sixty-two, sixty-three, sixty-four.'

'Don't . . .' Mia's face was frozen in horror.

We watched without speaking, and nine seconds later the shuttle blew apart in a vast ball of fire, the two boosters spiralling away on their own trajectories.

118

'You can change the channel and see the news flash hit. Or turn the radio on.' Demus sounded as sad about what had just happened as I felt.

Elton reached the TV in two strides and turned it off, angry. 'It's tricks. David freaking Copperfield stuff. If that guy can levitate over the Grand Canyon, then this guy here sure as hell can mess about with the timing on—'

'Messing about with time is exactly what I *am* doing, Elton.'

'Don't Elton me! You don't know me!'

'I do, though. I really do.' Demus still looked sad, almost as if he were on the edge of tears. He stepped in close to Elton, lowering his voice. 'I know exactly what you want to tell the others. And you should do it. A few decades from now, hardly anyone would bat an eyelid, Elton.' Demus pressed a folded piece of paper into his hand. 'Really. It all gets so much better.'

Elton stepped back as if stung, which wasn't Elton at all.

'I'm going to leave you to make your decisions,' Demus said. 'You'll do that better on your own. Nick can show me out.'

And, leaving a stunned silence in our wake, we both left the room. Demus moved confidently along the corridor toward the front door while I glanced around, expecting John's mum to appear and challenge us at any moment. We reached the door unscathed, though. Demus leaned in toward me as we stood outside on the steps.

'They'll talk about this as "saving Mia".' He shrugged. 'Let them. But you, you need to remember this: she saves you. In the end, she saves you. You're not rescuing a damsel in distress here. You're returning a favour in advance. She's special. Don't ever let me forget that.'

And with that he went.

I got back to the living room to find that John had got hold of a radio and turned the TV back on with the sound off. BBC 1 was breaking the news with footage of the explosion while on the radio an announcer was describing the scene.

I turned the radio down and eyed Elton, who had just sat down beside John. 'Well?'

Elton pursed his lips. He glanced down at the paper Demus had given him, then closed his hand around it. 'I can't argue. That man knows stuff he shouldn't be able to know.'

'Are we doing this thing, then?' I asked. 'Breaking in, going after the chip he needs?'

'We could try, I guess.' Elton stood again. 'Shit. I wouldn't have come if I'd've known what you were going to get me into.' He sat down again.

We spent maybe an hour just going over how crazy it all was. Trying to talk ourselves out of believing. And failing.

At last, John asked the other question. 'What was Demus talking about? He said you wanted to tell us something, Elton?'

'Yeah . . .' Elton took to his feet again, nervous once more. He manufactured a grin. 'Sorry I was late. I know you all wanted me to come and show you how to be cool with the ladies, but it seems like Mia got that sorted already.' He paused, still tense. Elton wasn't ever tense. He was the opposite of tense. He took tension out of you. 'And I know I was late for this man from the future shit that I still don't really believe but am going to act like I do believe anyhow . . .'

'What's up, Elton?' Mia looked at him curiously, like she knew something we didn't.

'Look. This party . . .' He sort of tossed his hands in the air and looked at the door.

'Just tell them,' Mia said.

'Well.' He puffed out his cheeks then took a deep breath. 'You ain't gonna see me getting off with no girls.'

I frowned. If I was honest, I didn't expect to see any of us getting off with a girl. Possibly John. But it wasn't as if we knew many people there. And Elton just wasn't bothered . . . 'I . . . Are you . . . ?'

'I wanted to invite you guys,' he said. 'It's important to me. And besides. You *really* need it. But it means now I gotta share more than I was . . . ready for.'

'You're gay!' I said. It all made sense. Suddenly the pieces fit together.

'No way.' John backed off a yard, laughing nervously. I could see all the thoughts crowding behind his eyes. Rock Hudson had died of AIDS a few months back. The newspapers were full of 'The Gay Plague'. At our school, nobody would ever come out and admit they were gay. Social suicide. It just wouldn't happen. Ever.

Simon just sat there looking slightly bored, as if we were talking about the weather.

'I needed to get that out there,' Elton said. 'That's how it is.' He slumped, but kept his chin up, eyes bright. 'I was going to say it. Demus just helped, is all.' He kept the crumpled paper tight in his fist as if it held a promise he wasn't going to let go of.

'I'm easy,' I said. 'Not that you were asking my permission.' A hasty addition, remembering quite how much even his 'play' punches hurt. At Maylert, we had the 'you're gay' jokes honed to a razor-edge. Perhaps it was the same at all boys' schools, a constant parade of protesting too much, all of us policing each other to a ridiculous degree in some kind of heartless dance of denial. I had to admit to taking part, and for all the hundreds of casual insults and accusations I'd flung, I had never truly thought any single one of them to be true, never believed a single one of my targets really gay. It was just part of the barbed and vicious banter of our existence. Some reflex part of me still wanted to riposte that it was good of him to leave more of the women to share around us real men. I bit back on it, knowing it to be small and petty. And realising with a breath of relief that saying something so stupid would have likely crashed any chances I had with Mia, who was watching me with unusual intensity. 'It . . . uh . . . can't have been easy to say. Thanks for trusting us.'

'Uh . . . yeah.' John nodded, his mouth twisting as he doubtless swallowed some of the same shit our school life had conditioned us with. 'You don't . . .' He looked around at Simon and me. 'You know?'

Elton sighed, and Mia rolled her eyes. 'You're a good-looking fellow, John, but you're really not my type.'

A silence drew out between us. Elton ended it. 'Questions?'

Another moment of silence, then Simon cleared his throat. 'I have one.' He eyed Elton up and down, speculatively. 'How are we going to get into this laboratory? Don't they have alarms and guard dogs and things? I'm not good with dogs.'

CHAPTER 16

I took a taxi to hospital for my last chemo session. Or, at least, the last one of this batch. The doctors said they would give me some time off to recover, then blast me with another course. I felt like an old tree in one of those late autumn gales. The chemo's job was to strip my leaves and keep them gone. My job was not to get uprooted while the gale blew.

Mother allowed me to go alone but promised to visit, despite my saying that she didn't have to. I wouldn't even be staying overnight. The doctors had had their fill of watching me puke and were ready to let me go home an hour after they'd filled my veins with their toxic waste.

I arrived to find Demus waiting for me on the steps outside, a cigarette in hand.

'You sure you're me? Didn't think I'd ever be stupid enough to smoke.' I went to join him, sitting upwind. Of course, the breeze changed immediately, swirling his fumes around me.

'Just trying new things, Nick.' He drew a lungful. 'It's not what it's cracked up to be . . . I wonder if crack is?'

'What?'

'I wonder if crack is what it's cracked up to be.'

'What's crack?'

'Never mind.' He waved the question away. 'So, are they up for this little robbery?'

'I think so. John wasn't happy about it. Or Elton. But they'll do it.'

'Good. Sunday is the time to aim for. Sunday night, or very early in the morning.' He reached for a supermarket bag at his feet and pulled out one of his headbands. 'The chip slots in here. I'm just using the databus and some core functions. And I've included a little instruction manual. Do break what will become the habit of our lifetime and actually read it.' He fished out a stapled pamphlet, then dropped it back in and took another drag on his cigarette. 'I mean, it's not awful or anything. I guess I just expected more from tobacco than it had to give . . . There's a lesson somewhere in there for you.'

'Except I'm not going to remember any lessons,' I said. 'Because you tell me that pretty soon I'm going to wipe out the memory of the last week. Come to think of it, if I wipe my memory, how did you remember to find me here or at John's the other day?'

Demus laughed. 'I don't remember the events, but I sure as hell remember the place and day of the week I had my chemo. And the guys are going to be talking for years to come about the dance lesson at John's on the day Demus predicted the Challenger disaster.'

I grunted my acknowledgment that he was right. 'Even so, I'm going to forget this lesson about smoking. *You* certainly did.'

'Well, yeah. There is that.' Demus nodded. He tapped the bag with his foot. 'The instructions for erasing are in the manual, too. It's a simpler process based around the application of powerful magnetic fields. No MiB shit here.'

'Em eye bee?'

'You know, *Men in Black*! Will Smith! What you think you saw, you did not see . . .' He trailed off. 'Sorry . . . Wrong decade. Anyway. Magnetic fields. A memory eraser. That's something you're going to have to develop in the next quarter-century, by the way.'

'Me? I don't do brains! Mathematics is—'

'You do brains. Trust me. I've included the basics at the back to start you off. Some time travel stuff, too.'

'That sounds a lot like cheating . . . Like cheating the universe!'

Demus shrugged. 'Meh. How do you think the universe got here? It pulled itself out of nothing by its own bootstraps. Happens all the time. Think of this as a little payback.' He straightened his leg and winced. 'I suspect that the self-seeding we're doing here accelerates science across a bunch of related areas. It's quite possible that the 2011 I've come back from is technologically a few decades ahead of where it would have been if I hadn't come back.'

'So we're literally changing the course of history?'

Demus shrugged.

'Over a girl?'

'There's a better reason?' He stubbed out his cigarette and smiled a slow smile. I found myself echoing it.

After a short silence, he continued, 'Anyway, technically we're changing the course of your future rather than my history. My history is fixed and unchangeable.' Demus tapped the bag again. 'These memory things raise almost as many questions as the time travelling, you know.' He handed me the carrier. It was far heavier than expected and I almost dropped it. 'I don't remember this last chemo session. Next month, you won't either. So, did the Nick who is going to suffer through it truly matter? Take it to a logical extreme. If I offered you a million pounds to endure a night of horrific but non-injuring torture, in the knowledge that the next day you could wipe out all memory of it . . . then Nick tomorrow would presumably be all for it. He would be a million pounds richer and perfectly happy. And the Nick who suffered so terribly . . . Where has he gone? The memories were just electro-chemical patterns that have been erased. The pain was just nerve impulses that have finished. And the Nick who screamed and begged for it to stop? Does he matter anymore? Did his agony matter? And if you say "yes", then repeat the question, but instead of a night of torture, reduce it to an hour, then a minute, then a second, then a quarter second. Does your opinion change?'

'I don't know.' I gripped the bag. The sheer weight of it felt important. As if it were telling me something.

'I don't know either, kid.' Demus got up to go.

'Wait.' I still had too many questions to know where to start, so I started with what scared me most and it wasn't the cancer. 'This psycho, Rust. If you're so keen to protect Mia, then shouldn't you do something about him? Somehow I don't think he's going to let this thing with her go.'

Demus winced as though just hearing the name hurt him. 'As soon as you get the chip, your Rust problem will go away.'

I blinked. 'You're going to wipe his memory, too?'

A half-smile. 'Just trust me.' He set a hand to my shoulder. 'Stay safe. And remember we're on a clock with this chip thing.'

'We are?' I shook my head. 'We need time to plan the raid. Scout the place out. Watch the guards. All that sort of thing. It's not like any of us are experts. There's no need to rush it.'

Demus let out a long sigh at my stupidity. 'I remember when I was you and a black BMW pulled up in front of me and Mia just after her mum cut Rust at the flat in the Miller Blocks. The next thing I remember is being in the park nearly two weeks later.'

'Ah.' I saw it then. 'We need the chip soon so I can forget everything from the BMW up to the park.' I really didn't want to forget dancing with Mia, or the upcoming party. 'Can't you just erase those days years later?'

He shook his head. 'Has to be done soon after they were formed, or you risk losing important stuff, like remembering how to eat or walk. You've got four days tops. Sorry about the timing. It wasn't mine to choose.'

He started to hobble off.

'Wait! When do I see you next?'

'Twenty-five years, for sure. Just look in the mirror. You'll see me coming.' He waved over his shoulder.

'You're bugging out? Seriously?'

'I don't know, Nick.' He turned, raising his voice to cover the growing gap. 'I don't remember.'

'You should come with us, help us get in and find the chip!'

'I don't think it happens that way, Nick.' He smiled though an air
of sadness hung around him. 'And I have other things to do.'

I watched me go, dogged by the feeling that there was something
important I was forgetting to ask him.

I got to the ward late and endured the tutting of Nurse Smithson as she
poked urgently in search of a vein. When at last I was plumbed in, I sat
in the chair beside my allotted bed and fished out one of the books I'd
bought. There would be time for Demus's toys and instructions later. I
was still irked that he'd left me the task of inventing the damn things.
Like an exercise for the student.

I thumbed through my big fat copy of *The Lord of the Rings* to
where I'd left the page folded. It was a comfort read. I knew the story
backwards. For a quarter of an hour or so Tolkien had my full attention. Hobbits, elves, a king without a crown. A quest focused on a small
but crucial object about which the world unknowingly revolved. But
with the turning of each page, I felt a scraping at the back of my mind.
Not an irritation, not something that was there and shouldn't be, but
the absence of something, like the missing tick of a loud clock that has
finally wound down. I set the book beside me.

'Where's Eva?'

In the bed next door, David rolled my way. He was fourteen and had
also been a target for Eva's stream of consciousness oversharing. 'ICU.'

'Hell.' When I'd first heard that term I understood it as 'I see you.'
But the acronym stood for Intensive Care Unit, and it wasn't a place
you wanted anyone to see you.

'Where you going?' David sat up as I got to my feet.

'Checking on her, of course.' I pushed my drip stand ahead of me. It was on a splayed foot set with six caster wheels and should have been easy to steer. Instead, like every supermarket trolley ever, it wanted to veer into any given obstacle.

I reached the nurses' station at the entrance to the ward and answered the expectant gaze of the woman on duty with a lie. 'I think there's something wrong with David. He's frothing at the mouth.'

As she hurried to investigate, I left the ward unhindered.

The good thing about hospitals is that they're always full of directions. I took the lift to the sixth floor and followed the signs to the ICU. I drew the occasional glance in my hospital gown with accompanying chemo takeout, but nobody challenged me.

Getting into the ICU was a matter of timing. I had to wait almost half an hour for my moment, which was also long enough to be sure that David hadn't grassed me up, since nobody came to collect me.

The number of nurses at a nurses' station is governed by a well-known mathematical distribution named after Siméon Denis Poisson and demonstrated by him in 1837. It was famously used to describe and predict the number of cadets kicked to death by their horses at a Prussian military academy, but it works equally well for nurses. Random events conspire to call the nurses from their station, and if you bide your time, the number on duty will eventually be zero.

I walked in past the empty reception, checked the board beside it and found that Eva Schwartz was in Room 5, then proceeded toward her door.

I pushed into the room. It felt as though it should have been darkened but it wasn't. Painfully bright hospital lights picked out every detail in harsh relief. Machines crowded the room, more of them than they could possibly be using. A sats monitor charted respirations, blood O_2, and heart rate, a cylinder dispensed oxygen along a plastic tube, a drip stand offered intravenous fluids, other tubes drained the excess, additional leads made their enquiries and reported to boxes of electronics all humming and beeping to themselves. The room was white. Too white. The sheets could star in any washing powder commercial. And, in their midst, staining their perfection, the uncooperative human stubbornly dying amid this array of cleverness and invention.

Eva looked very small in that bed. Very alone in that room among the gently murmuring medical equipment.

I navigated a path around the various stands to crouch in her eye line. She wasn't asleep, but I couldn't tell if she saw me. 'Hey.' I thought I should have more to say. If not me, then who? We were walking down the same path. 'Eva . . .'

She studied me from some distant place, her dark eyes hardly moving. Her cracked lips made no attempt at words.

'Look . . . I . . .' I pulled up a plastic chair almost identical to the ones at school and winced at the scraping noise. I sat where she could see me. 'I've been caught up in my own stuff, Eva. And I'm sorry. I should have been a better . . . person . . . better friend. I've been rude when I should have been kind. You wanted someone to hear you. We all do really.'

I watched her, and she watched me back, a papery residue of dried saliva on her dry lips. 'They'll come and take me out of here soon enough, I guess.' I glanced at the door. 'I'm not used to being the one doing the talking here.' I tried a smile, but it hurt my face. There was an ache in my chest from emotions that wouldn't fit right. Some of it was the self-pity that Demus had refused to show me. 'I don't know if it helps, Eva, but . . . there's so much more to this world than I ever thought there was . . .' I bit my lip and thought of the worlds splitting away from us at every moment in infinite profusion. There were an infinity of Evas living every kind of life. Evas who survived her cancer, Evas who never got cancer in the first place, Evas who got killed in a car crash on their way to the diagnosis, Evas who flourished and realised their ambitions, and grew fat and old and happy. Every possibility probed. The good and the bad. I didn't know if it mattered. All

I cared about was the Eva in front of me, her breath rattling in, rattling out, her heart beating across a screen.

I understood then why Demus needed me to be him, needed my Mia to be his Mia. We might live in a multiverse of infinite wonder, but we are what we are, and can only care about what falls into our own orbit. 'I guess I'm just saying that none of us really know what's going on or why, and that we never know what's happening or where we're going.' I was babbling and knew it. I took her hand and the smallest smile reached her mouth.

The door opened, and a dark-haired nurse hissed at me. 'You need to come out of there. Right now.'

'I'm staying until her parents come.' I took tight hold of the bed rail, then met the woman's stare. 'And you can't make me leave.'

CHAPTER 17

The night after my last session of chemo was the night of the Arnots'
party. John phoned me four times between getting home from school
and coming over.

'What are you wearing?' That was the first call.

'Uh. Clothes?' I hadn't given the matter any thought at all.

'Duh. But what clothes?'

'The ones I'm wearing.'

'*Really?*' He managed to put enough doubt into a single word to
make me question myself. And he hadn't even seen what I was wearing.

'No, you're right, I'm going to change into spandex and those glam
rock trousers I have to oil my legs to get into.'

' . . . '

'Jeans and a T-shirt. Now get your arse over here, because we might
have to abduct Simon.'

The next call was about booze.

'Can you get a bottle of red and two bottles of white?'

'Wine? John, your father has a fucking cellar full of the stuff.' I'd been down there. There were literally thousands of bottles. Several dozen of them dust-laden vintages from the 1930s.

'Yeah, but he's wised-up to me taking it. There's a combination lock on the door now!'

I glanced toward the living room where Mother was reading and lowered my voice to a hiss. 'If you can't crack his wine cellar, it doesn't bode well for breaking into his secure laboratory!'

'Just get some plonk, will you. And some beer. Don't want to look too posh.'

'I'll see what I can do.' I put the phone down with a sigh. Successful booze buying depended on the right pantomime. I had, for example, been buying my mother a bottle of Bailey's Irish Cream every year for the last six or seven years without any parental input. She loved the stuff, but didn't trust herself to buy it, and so birthdays were a doddle. And when a ten-year-old boy walks into an off-licence, where they all know him, to buy a bottle of creamy liqueur, there's no problem. If a fifteen-year-old with greasy hair and scrubbed-down acne tries to buy a six-pack of Special Brew . . . very different story.

The place for a teenager to buy beer was the supermarket. But you had to pad your basket out sufficiently to prove you were there on parents' orders. For best results, take a shopping list on which the beers are written, and sandwich them between a bag of frozen peas and some fish fingers. The true artist invests in some female sanitary products, too.

The next call came ten minutes after the time that John had sworn he would arrive by.

'Did you get it?'

'Cheap wine, check. Expensive beer, check.' I'd taken off the hat to exploit any sympathy on offer. I don't know if I got any, but the teller couldn't see me through her checkout fast enough. 'Fish fingers, check. Baked beans, check. Card for Henri, check.'

'What?'

'It's his twenty-first. I got him a card.'

'I guess.'

'So, where are you?'

'High Street. I'm trying to get some condoms, but . . . I don't suppose you—'

I hung up. Yes, I had to admire the lofty heights of his optimism. No, I wasn't going to buy them for him if he was too chicken.

The last call came when he was half an hour late.

'I'm leaving! I'm leaving!'

'You're back at your house?'

'No, I'm leaving. Pay attention.'

'Leaving your house?'

'I'm heading for the door. The phone cord won't stretch much further! Cover your ears. When it pings back it's going to make a hell of a—'

John arrived an hour late.

'What? Nobody is ever on time for a party.'

'My mum's giving us a lift to Simon's. We'll probably walk from there.'

John shrugged then spread his arms and beckoned my attention with wafting fingers.

'Very nice,' I said without enthusiasm. He had on a baseball jacket he bought in the States, white and red suede, sporting a large 41. Black trousers and shiny leather shoes. 'You'll be able to talk to all the girls about that time you went to America.' He also appeared to have showered in aftershave, possibly hoping that the fumes would overwhelm the object of his affections and leave her unable to resist his attentions.

Mother poked her head out of the living room. 'Hello, John. You're looking very dapper.'

'Thanks, Mrs H.'

Mother frowned at that. 'Are we ready to go?'

I picked up the booze bag, each of its contents individually wrapped in a shirt to stop any clinking or clanking. I hoped that when I said 'party' Mother's imagination still ran to images of the ones I went to when I was eleven. 'I'm staying over at John's, remember?'

'I know.' Mother gathered her car keys. 'And John, don't let him overdo it. He really should be in bed by ten.'

I made no protest. If you've no intention of obeying, then why not agree. Besides, I felt pretty rough. I could see myself wanting my bed by ten.

Simon's mother greeted us conspiratorially at the door. 'He's pretending to have forgotten all about it, and is also claiming a cold. Take no excuses. I'm depending on you boys.'

We clumped up the stairs in our shoes.

'Up and at 'em, Si!'

'Party! Party!'

Simon came to his bedroom door wrapped in a blanket, sniffing.

'I like it! Great poncho!' John took hold of one arm.

'I see the plan is to jump a whole bunch of bases and get the girls under your covers in one step.' I took the other arm.

'Wait! I'm ill!' He backpedalled and started to win. Heavy people can do that.

'No.' I pulled off my woollen hat exposing my baldness. '*I'm* ill. You're just antisocial.'

That at least stopped him reversing.

'You're doing this to keep Mia at the D&D table,' John said. 'Remember?'

Simon exhaled his defeat and slumped.

'Come along with us, say hi to Elton, wish his brother a happy birthday. Swig a coke. Dance if you want to. Duty done. You can come home.'

'Alright.' And Simon let us lead him down the stairs as though he were walking the last mile on death row.

The walk to the Arnots' flat was long, cold, and dark. We talked about the microchip more than about the party. John had found his father's list of passwords with astonishing ease. They were written on a piece of paper folded into his wallet and helpfully labelled 'passwords'. He had seven of them and Simon surmised that he was probably just given them because of his seniority, as a backup in case of emergency. As far as John knew, his father couldn't tell one end of a computer from the other.

'He sometimes needs help using his programmable calculator, and I know for a fact that's one calculator that has never had a program written on it!'

We crossed the Arnots' local high street, a parade of smaller shops with a pub at each end. A figure detached itself from the blackness outside The Spotted Horse as we approached.

'They let you little ones out after dark then?' Ian Rust tilted his head in question. The lamplight painted his hollow face in shadows. Beneath his right eye, an angry three-inch scar ran parallel to his cheekbone.

None of us spoke.

'Heard you kicked a friend of mine, Hayes.' Rust showed his teeth. Perhaps he thought he was smiling. I doubted that he really knew what a friend was. 'I want hold of that girl you were with. My Mia. She's been keeping a low profile. But you know where she is, don't you, Nicky?'

'I've not seen her.' My voice shook.

Rust's smile broadened. 'You'll tell me, Hayes. Little Nicky Hayes. Number 18 Redhill Road. Minus one father. Not feeling too well of late.'

'Fuck off.' I realised that it was John who'd said it. It was pretty much the bravest thing I'd ever seen.

'I'm bigger than you.' It wasn't exactly witty, but he had called me Little Nicky, and I couldn't leave John hanging.

Simon kept his eyes firmly on the ground, frowning intensely, but he did step up to take his place between us.

Rust's impression of a smile slipped just the smallest fraction. I imagined that behind those shark-dead eyes of his he might be considering just knifing all three of us as a serious option. A bunch of men chose that moment to emerge from The Spotted Horse, light and laughter spilling into the street with them. Rust snarled, and instead of attacking he sketched a bow.

'Ladies.' He waved us on. 'I've got a busy night planned. Can't stop to play just now. Catch you later.'

We walked a hundred yards before anyone spoke. 'Is he following us?' Simon asked.

I looked back. I was still trembling. Ready to fight or run, with heavy odds on the running. 'No.'

'Jesus! I may need a new pair of trousers.' John shook his head. 'I just told the worst head-case in the school to fuck himself. I'm dead.'

'He's not in school anymore,' Simon said. 'He got expelled. For pulling a knife on a teacher.'

'Thanks, Simon, for that helpful reminder.'

'We're with you.' I tried to sound confident.

'OK . . . *we're* dead.' John started walking again, picking up the pace. 'C'mon. This makes it even more important that I get laid quickly.'

We felt the pulse of the beat before we saw the crowd outside the Arnots' flat. We threaded our way through the guests who'd already had enough dancing and drinking to weather the cold and inserted ourselves through the open door. One of the middle Arnot brothers was watching the entrance: Marc, a man of few words and packed with muscle, but always with a smile ready behind a stern exterior. He waved us through, and moments later we were wedging our way into the kitchen to unload our offerings.

The entire ground floor of the flat would have fitted inside either of the two living rooms John had entertained us in a few days earlier. Even so, somehow dozens of people were in the main room, dancing or chilling at the edges. Lionel Richie surrendered to the Pointer Sisters who began to declare, in no uncertain terms, just how excited they were. We took beers from the sideboard and tried to look as if we knew what we were doing.

It wasn't the music I listened to in my room. It lacked the uptight, self-deprecating introspective angst of my chosen groups, but God, it made you want to dance. The heat made me thirsty and the can gave me something to do with my hands. It was empty before I knew it.

Fingers tugged at my sleeve. 'Hi!' Mia in her war-paint, smiling.

'Hey.' I had to fit the word past the music.

She introduced us to the two girls who had pressed in behind her. I didn't hear their names. I shouted some inane small talk at her, but, thankfully, it didn't register over the beat.

Mia gestured with her head to the middle of the room. 'Come on.' At least that's what my lip-reading skills suggested she had said. She set a small hand behind my elbow and I let myself be steered away from the wall.

The night of Henri Arnot's twenty-first was the night I discovered how a large amount of music and a modest amount of beer could take five hours and zip them past you like an express train. My body, which had protested bitterly about walking the two miles from Simon's to Elton's, didn't so much as murmur a complaint about sweating through a night's dancing. I guess every generation thinks it's born into the golden age of music, but that night it was easy to believe that nobody had had it as good as we did. Chaka Khan let us rock her, Grand Master Flash and the Furious Five had white lines for us to follow, and Frankie Goes To Hollywood demanded that we 'Relax'.

'Where's Simon?' I steered John away from the pair of Mia's friends who seemed to be in competition for his affections.

'Crashed.' John nodded to the darkest corner where Simon's head could just be seen emerging from a pile of coats. He was fast asleep.

One of the girls reclaimed John, and I found my way back to the kitchen, floating on a beer buzz and dance high. I felt rather like a stray helium balloon drifting on the currents. The kitchen was crowded, though less so than the living room, and with an older demographic. Elton's dad stood with his back to a counter strewn with mostly empty bowls of crisps and small plates of twiglets, a foodstuff so disgusting that it was always the last to go at any party.

'Nick. How you doing?' Elton's dad spoke with a deep French-Madagascan accent that I had to focus on to unravel.

'Good, thanks.' I grinned. 'Great.'

'Good.'

Like all of my friends' dads, with the recent exception of John's, I didn't know his name or what he did, but I knew he was old, older than Mother, older than Demus; hair thinning and speckled with white, face lined and tired. And I knew that nearly fifteen years ago he had, at the general invitation of the British government, got on a boat in Port Suarez with his pregnant wife and four tiny sons, and spent weeks sailing toward our cold, wet island. And he'd made a home here, built a life, watched his children grow.

'Mr Arnot . . .' I realised that I was drunk and made an effort not to slur.

'Jean,' he said, offering a slow smile and nodding to someone passing.

'Jean,' I said. 'Thank you. For this.' I waved an arm at the party and was lucky not to spill anyone's drink.

He shrugged. 'My eldest boy is twenty-one.'

I found myself seized by a sudden desire to pontificate on the nature of the universe, which to be fair I had found out an awful lot about recently. Instead, I asked a question. 'What . . . ? I mean, you've been around . . . What's the most important piece of advice you'd give Henri? Y'know. About living.' I restrained myself from a second arm wave.

Elton's father smiled, as if the fundamental questions of life were common fare among boys with too much beer in them. He beckoned me closer and I leaned in.

'Kiss the girl.'

'That's it?' I frowned. I had hoped for some deeper wisdom that might help me unravel the conundrums of infinitely many universes and man's relationship with time and memory.

'Kiss the girl.' He nodded and the man beside him laughed.

'Thanks.' I claimed a plastic cup containing an unknown dark liquid and began to drift back toward the living room. The hall clock amazed me with the claim that it was a little after two in the morning. Lionel Richie had reclaimed the record player and slowed the dance floor to a shuffle that required two to play.

'Hello,' Mia echoed Lionel, threading her hand into mine. I found somewhere to leave my cup, and moments later we joined the couples rocking slowly around the room.

Slow dancing is basically communal cuddling, and right then it was the best thing ever to happen to me. When Mia pressed herself against me, the tiredness of five hours of dancing, the weight of an unknown volume of beer, and the burden of my illness all fell away as if a dial had been turned to a new setting.

I saw, over Mia's head, that John was currently locked in the arms of her friend, unable to catch my eye as his face appeared to be welded to the girl's. I bent to mention the hot news to Mia and found her face raised to mine, my lips approaching her mouth rather than her ear. *Kiss the girl.*

Despite John's endless prepping I was still taken unawares when Mia's lips met mine only briefly, to be replaced by the questing warmth of her tongue. Immediately, we were kissing as if both of us were starving and the other was our only nourishment. It felt less real than, and far more exciting than talking to my own future self. A kind of cool electric fire ran through every vein. I was suddenly alive with a fierceness I hadn't imagined possible, damned if I would let a tiny error in my DNA poison my blood and take this from me. I felt invincible. Unstoppable . . . Mia stopped me. She pulled back with an unreadable smile and smeared lipstick. 'The song's over.'

CHAPTER 18

'Christ! It's gone three.'

A cruel turning on of the main lights had driven the partygoers from the Arnots' flat, and we now stood in the freezing night a few yards from the front door, the crowd around us dispersing with drunken goodbyes.

'We'll walk you home,' I told Mia. John nodded, having finally disentangled himself from the girl he'd hooked up with. Simon just stood there yawning, bleary eyed. I'm not convinced he really knew where he was.

Mia shrugged as if it wasn't necessary, but she also took my hand and laced her fingers with mine. She returned my idiot grin with one of her small but delicious smiles. We set off hand in hand, John and Simon following along behind.

By the time we reached the end of the road, John was halfway through a passable rendition of Michael Jackson's 'Thriller' and my thoughts were firmly on the goodnight kiss waiting for me outside Mia's door.

The throaty growl of a car engine turned us around. The headlights flicked on, freezing us in full beam. The car had pulled out behind us from the opposite side of the road. Squinting, all I could see was a black paintjob and sleek sporty lines. I thought it might be Demus again in his BMW.

The driver door opened and a figure emerged. 'I told you I'd catch you later.'

Mia and I dropped each other's hand like naughty children caught in the act.

Ian Rust reached in to dip the headlights of his undoubtedly stolen car. 'Mia is coming with me.' He stepped into the light, dishevelled and with a dark stain on his upper arm as though he'd been cut. Splatters across his shirt lower down looked as if they might be someone else's blood. Simon took to his heels.

Rust craned his neck to one side then glanced after our retreating friend. 'I would love it if you'd try to stop me. The night's young yet, and I'm only getting started.'

'I've paid Sacks,' Mia said, trying to sound confident. 'He's good with it.'

'But I,' Rust said, 'am not good with Sacks. I feel it's time for a change of management. Which means, you owe me.'

'How much?' I asked. It took an effort to get the question past my lips. To draw those wicked little eyes my way.

'How much have you got, Hayes?' Something in his tone told me that whatever I offered wouldn't be enough. This wasn't about money. It was about power and control. Rust had seen something in Mia that he wanted to own. He started a slow advance, daring us to run.

'The police are after you,' John said.

The three of us backed up a pace for each one Rust advanced, maintaining a five-yard gap.

'If they want me, here I am.' Rust spread his arms and devoured a yard in one swift stride. I lurched back like a frightened animal, nearly falling on my arse. I'd heard that alcohol gave you courage, but the beers I'd consumed, against medical advice, didn't seem to be working.

Whatever John had been drinking seemed to be working fine, however. Instead of stumbling back he threw himself at Rust, as if he didn't believe the stories we all knew were true. Rust swayed to the left and somehow John went crashing by, impacting noisily against the side of the stolen car.

'Come on.' Rust beckoned to Mia. 'Or do I have to start breaking pretty boy here?' He glanced back at John, on all fours by the car, groggy and groaning. A swift kick to the ribs laid John flat on the road. 'Well?'

Shouts and the sound of running feet saved Mia from answering. Elton and two of his brothers were speeding toward us, others behind them, Simon far to the rear, but puffing gamely back down the street.

Marc and Henri reached us first, Elton close behind. Amazingly, Rust seemed unfazed. Without hurrying he stepped back toward John, grasped a handful of his hair and dragged him to his feet. A few other guys from the party arrived, Simon bringing up the rear. Rust kicked the back of John's knee and held him from behind by chin and hair as he knelt in the road. John's breath came in short panting gasps. He was properly scared of the monster now. Blood from a cut on his forehead ran in trickles down into his eye. Rust looked pointedly at Mia. 'Get in the car.'

Elton and his brothers advanced. 'Let him go, or—'

'Or what?' Rust sneered. 'Think you can stop me snapping his neck?' He shook his head. 'Mia knows what to do.'

I stood frozen by fear. Rust had something broken inside him. You could see it in his face. A hole in his mind that needed to be filled with other people's pain. He was burning his bridges just for the joy of seeing the flames take them. He would break John's neck without hesitation. He'd do it and walk off, leaving my friend paralysed, a life taken away, replaced by long years of helpless dependence.

'Let him go.' Mia bowed her head and started to walk toward the passenger door. That's when a dark shape loomed up behind Rust, pulled his arm back, and in the blink of an eye had him over the car bonnet with the captured arm twisted behind his back.

While Elton and others moved quickly to help John away, I just stood there blinking stupidly at Mr Arnot, who had circled round and walked calmly up behind Rust to put him in an arm lock.

When Mia and John were safe with the rest of us, behind a wall of the Arnots and their relatives, Mr Arnot released his snarling prisoner and stepped smartly away to join us.

Rust whipped around, a blade gleaming in his hand, and for a moment it looked as if he might just hurl himself into the midst of us. He managed to contain his fury and instead held his knife out at arm's length, sighting down the edge at Mr Arnot as he backed away. 'You, old man. You put your *dirty* hands on me. I can't be having that.' His voice shook with loathing and with a tightly bound rage. 'You watch yourself, old man, because I might just have to find you one night and cut an apology out of you.'

As one, we all began to retreat back up the street. Rust watched us hungrily as if looking for stragglers.

'He's mad.' John wiped the blood from his eye.

'Looney tunes.' Elton glanced back. 'Dangerous. You keep away from that guy.'

'No kidding,' I said. 'We should call the police.'

'That one will find them soon enough,' Henri said behind us.

'Your dad's really something!' Mia raised her voice and called out, 'Thanks, Mr Arnot!' Ahead of us Mr Arnot raised a hand in acknowledgement. 'I didn't know he could handle himself like that.'

Elton nodded, a touch of pride in his face. 'Who do you think got us all into martial arts? He's old now, but still tough. Used to box back in Madagascar. He does security work these days.'

We headed back toward the warmth and light of the Arnots' flat, marvelling at Rust's craziness. I just listened, very tired now. Walking along in the cold night it occurred to me that, in the great multitude of humanity, creatures like Ian Rust were like the cancer cells among the crush of blood cells in my veins. Rare, but requiring only one to begin to pollute everything around them. Because ugliness multiplies, and hurt spills over into hurt, and sometimes good things are just the fuel for evil's fire. I found myself limping, all my pains returning, the weight of my illness settling on me, too heavy to be borne. Two more steps might have seen me falling to my knees. But Mia's hand found mine, our fingers laced, and I walked on feeling that I could go all night.

CHAPTER 19

We came to D&D late, with thick heads. John, sporting an impressive scar on his forehead, seemed inordinately pleased with himself, though unable to remember the walk back to Simon's house during which he had danced with lampposts, climbed over a Mercedes, and declared from its roof his love for the girl he had been dancing with.

'Lisa! Lovely Lisa!' he'd crooned, sliding back to the pavement.

'Wasn't that one called Laura?' Simon had asked, puffing steam before him as he kept up.

'Um . . .'

Mia came in with Elton, last as always. She flashed me a small smile and a knowing look. We had left her at the Arnots' and parted without words the night before. I had no idea what to expect this morning. Was she my girlfriend now? Did I have to play it cool and keep my distance? I wished Demus had thought to include that in his little how-to manuals. All I knew was that I had sore lips, my jaw ached, and I wanted to kiss her again. Then some more.

Elton, who never drank, flashed a bright smile at us. 'Boys! Ready to play?'

'Sure.' I slipped myself one of Simon's mum's indigestion tablets and drank some of the milk I'd asked for. 'The big question, though, is are we ready for tomorrow night?'

The others frowned at that as if it had been a troubling thought they'd managed successfully to push to a forgotten corner of their minds.

'I believe him and all,' said John. 'But this accident Mia's supposed to have isn't for twenty something years. That's a lot of time to think of an alternative . . . Sorry Mia.'

'No problem,' Mia said. 'If I understood what he said, then that Mia who gets hurt doesn't even have to be me . . .'

Elton nodded uncertainly. I was losing them.

It was Simon who turned the tide. 'We need to do it for Mia and Nick.'

'Nick? What's it got to go with Nick?' Elton asked.

'Well, Demus is a future Nick,' Simon said, as if it were obvious.

'He's what?' Mia shot an accusing look at me. The other two let their jaws drop.

Simon carried on, oblivious. 'So if we do what Demus remembers, then we make sure Demus isn't just any old future Nick, we make him *our* Nick. And that means that Nick beats his leukaemia and lives to be at least forty. Which isn't very likely if he just takes his chances.'

'Demus is you?' Mia asked, still shocked.

I didn't answer. I could see that they all knew he was, now that Simon had said it. They were probably wondering how they could possibly have not seen it before.

'So we're doing it,' said Simon. 'For Nick and for Mia. Right?'

'If it has to be.' Elton bowed his head.

Mia nodded, though the look she gave me said that there would be more to come from her on the subject of Demus.

John nodded too. 'We're going to get caught.' He rolled a couple of dice as if that might determine our fate.

'We might have to run. We shouldn't get caught, not unless we're stupid.' Elton frowned. 'I told you my dad does security work. He works nights for an agency. He says it's all about protecting the sites.

They're not interested in actually catching you. The police get the brownie points for that, and the pay, not the security guards.'

'What about dogs?' Simon returned to his big fear.

'They use them on building sites and things like that where there's valuable equipment lying around. Not indoors. Nobody wants to come back to dog crap on the carpet in the morning.'

'But—'

'Are we here to play, or what?' Elton readied his books, standing some up as a shield to his notes.

We chorused our yeses. We all wanted to think about imaginary dangers for a bit rather than real ones.

He leaned over the table and set something on the table before us: a cylinder woven from red and white ribbons of leather or plastic, about as wide as a finger and maybe five inches long.

'Don't touch it!' Simon slapped at Mia's hand as she started to reach.

'Ow!' She drew back, scowling. 'Why not?'

'It's something Elton does,' I said. 'He'll put things there and, if you touch them, it triggers something in the game. Never something good. He put a glass of coke there once and I swigged from it. That's how my first character died. Poisoned rations. Me drinking the coke put my guy in the frame as the first one to eat them. Failed my saving throw. Dead.'

Mia nodded. 'No touching.' A small grin my way. Did it mean she'd forgiven me already?

She pushed the three pieces of paper from the last session out across the table. 'Fort. Two. Sicker.' The words of wisdom her character's god had sent her when called upon for advice about saving us. I could see some sense in them: there were two of us who were sick, my Nicodemus and Mia's priestess, both turning grey and fading from the world. We were getting sicker, and it had happened beneath the fort. But how this constituted divine guidance, I had no idea. It made Demus seem like a plain speaker.

'Maybe it's an anagram,' Simon said.

'Why would my god send me an anagram?' Mia asked.

Simon shrugged. 'Elton likes them.'

'Hmmm.' Mia moved the pieces of paper around. 'You work on that then. And we'll get on with . . . what were we doing again?'

'Trekking endlessly into an endless wasteland.' John sighed.

'And fading,' Simon added helpfully.

'It's true, the cleric and Nicodemus are both getting pretty faint,' Elton said. 'You could probably get work as ghosts. You look kinda like someone could push a stick through you without causing too many problems.'

We kept heading out into the wastes, without a map or any direction other than the one that Mia's prayer had squeezed out of the Man Jesus. Water began to run low, rations lower.

'Another morning rolls around. No breakfast. More belt tightening.' Elton threw some dice to see if anything bad wandered our way. I rather looked forward to a monster hoving into view: it would be a bit of excitement, and plus we could eat it. A self-delivering meal. But nothing came. 'Be right back.' Elton drained his coke and headed off to the loo.

The moment the door closed behind him, Mia reached for the cylinder he'd set on the table.

'Mia!' I hissed. I had to admit, though, that the thing had been tempting me all morning. There's nothing like being told you can't touch something to make you want to touch it.

'It's nothing. Just a flexible tube.' She fiddled with it, getting the compulsion out of her hands.

'Make sure you put it back in exactly the same place,' John hissed.

'And quickly!' Simon pointed at the door as if Elton was about to burst back through it at any moment.

'Oh . . .' Mia looked up, frowning.

'What? Have . . .'

She held out her hands. Somehow, she had contrived to stick her index fingers into either end of the tube. Across the landing came the sound of a toilet flushing.

'Quick! Put it back!'

'I . . . It's stuck!' Mia appeared to be tugging, the tube stretching and narrowing between her fingers.

'Stop messing about,' Simon snarled.

'I'm not. It won't come off! I'm stuck—'

The door opened and Elton walked in, grinning from ear to ear. 'I love it when a plan comes together.' He sat down and picked up his notes. 'The ground starts to shake. Small stones dance on the hardpan. Dust lifts around your ankles. You feel the vibrations through the soles of your boots. The ground starts to break. The— Yes, Fineous?'

Simon lowered his hand. 'Fineous starts to run.'

'In any particular direction?'

'Away?'

'It's happening all around, as far as you can see.'

'Fineous stays where he is, then, and starts to limber up in preparation for running.'

'Fine. The ground starts to heave and all around you, in a vast circle, a wall of reddish brown stone rises, shedding earth. And as you spin to take it all in you see a tower emerging at the centre, maybe quarter of a mile from you. A great stone spike. It's already a hundred feet high.'

'Can we get over this wall?' Simon asked.

'By the time you reach it, it's over your head.'

'I could climb it?'

'It stops growing with a jolt, like a bolt being slammed home. The tower is still rising behind you. The wall is twenty yards high. Sheer stone.'

'Can you get this damn thing off me?' Mia thrust her hands toward me, the tube still taut between straining fingers. 'It's freaking me out.'

'Stop pulling,' John said. 'I remember now. I've seen these before. Chinese finger traps.'

'You could have said earlier!' I shook my head.

'Hey, I was up all night snogging.' John grinned. 'And, besides, the one I saw didn't look the same.'

'Alright. I don't care. How do I get out?' Mia had stopped pulling.

'That I don't remember,' John said.

I took Mia's hands, glad of the excuse, holding them with more familiarity than I would have before the party. 'Well . . .' I could see how the weave of the material tightened the tube about her fingertips. 'It's not like there are many options . . .'

'Scissors!' Mia said.

'Hey! No scissors!' Elton started from his chair.

'I . . . Try pushing your fingers together,' I suggested.

'Together? But I . . . Oh!' Mia followed my suggestion even as she objected to it, and in moments she was free.

'Fineous will try to climb the wall.' Simon reached for his dice.

'Sure.' Elton nodded. 'But there is a gate about fifty yards to the right of you.' He drew a circle for the wall. A smaller one inside for the tower. And added a door to both.

'I'll go to the door,' John said. The rest of us followed.

'There's an old man standing before it. Brown robe, long reddish beard. It'd probably be white if it wasn't covered in dust.'

'Where are we?' I asked. 'I ask the guy.'

'You, young man,' Elton did a querulous old voice, 'are at the Tower of Tricks.'

'Got it.' Simon reached for the pieces of paper. 'Two. Sicker. Fort. It's Tower of Tricks. I told you he loves anagrams.'

'We need to get these two cured.' John pointed at Mia and me. 'How can we do that?'

'Just leave. Nothing that you do not desire can leave with you.'

'That's it. We can just walk out of here and leave our woes behind us?'

Elton nodded, the tentative movement of an old man with a dust-laden beard. He gestured with one hand toward the imagined door.

'Ohhh kaaaaaay . . .' John pushed the lead figure representing his warrior toward the door.

'Wait.' Mia reached out to stop him. 'It can't be this easy.'

'It is the Tower of Tricks . . .' I said. 'It *could* be this easy.'

'Or . . .' Mia tapped the table. 'There could be a trick to leaving. Like the finger trap. When I tried the obvious way, I just got held harder. I had to push deeper in to get out.' She turned to Elton. 'I ask the old guy whether the door in the wall will really let us out, or if we need to go into the Tower of Tricks to get free.'

Elton creaked out an answer in his old man's voice. 'You're already in the Tower. We all are. We were born in it and nobody ever gets out of it alive.'

'And that?' Mia tapped the circle at the centre of the map. 'If we go in there, can we come out again and leave our disease behind us?'

Elton shrugged. 'You can try. If you emerge from the physical tower that you can see, you will be shriven, free of all curses and evils set upon you. But the Tower will not want to let go of you once you step inside. Nobody escapes that building without sacrifice, and often the sacrifice is greater than the benefit they sought. It's a trick . . . you see.' He manufactured an apologetic smile.

'Well.' I pushed the figure representing Nicodemus forward. 'Mia and I have to go in.' I looked at her. 'Coming?' It was more than an invitation to pit herself against a tower full of fiendish traps. 'Are you with me, Mia?'

A smile. One of those small, wicked grins of hers that lit me up. 'Sure.' She advanced her priest and at the same time pressed her leg against mine under the table.

A foolish grin spread across my face. 'Perhaps you guys should wait outside?'

John rolled his eyes and pushed his warrior forward. 'One for all.'

'And all for one,' Simon said with less enthusiasm. He pushed Fineous to the rear of our little group.

The afternoon progressed with us working our way up the tower through ever more fiendish death traps. Hours escaped, but we didn't. Though we did rise steadily higher.

'You've got a gift for death traps, Elton.' John crossed off the supplies he'd used up helping us escape the last one, a black sphere that pursued us, devouring everything it touched except the walls of the tower itself. We finally figured that as it ate, it grew, and we proceeded to feed it everything we could spare, and quite a lot that we couldn't, until it became too large to fit through the doorways and could be left behind.

'How far up this tower are we?' I asked.

Elton shrugged.

'You said there were windows,' Simon said. 'Fineous looks out of one. Carefully!'

'You're careful enough to avoid being beheaded by one of the steel rings that encircle the tower and rise and fall at speed. The tower stretches up above you, until it's lost in the clouds.'

'Shit.'

'Maybe we're doing it wrong,' Mia said. 'The old man said nobody leaves without sacrifice.'

'I've sacrificed loads!' John pointed irritably to the dozen items crossed off his character sheet.

'Maybe it wants more?' Mia suggested. 'Perhaps if the traps had got us, then that would have counted. Maybe we should just say that we're ready to make the sacrifice?'

'Really?' Elton used his old voice and produced the figure he had used for the man at the gate, now setting it behind Mia.

'I guess . . .' She looked around at us.

We grunted our agreement.

"'On your heads be it," the old man says. He raises both arms and darkness swirls around you.' Elton rolled his dice in secret. 'John, you need to go downstairs for a bit. Go bother Baggage.'

John sighed and left the room clutching his character sheet.

Elton looked serious. 'You're all in a stone walled room with one iron door. Except for John. You can see him through a window in the rear wall. He's in an identical room, but he doesn't seem to be able to see or hear you. You three have your ankles bound together with chains and are positioned by the wall between the two rooms. John's warrior isn't tied and is standing by the exit to his room.

'The old man is with you. He says that if one door is opened, then the other door will lock permanently, and not only that, the floor of the other room will vanish and that the drop beneath is fatal.'

'Break the glass!' I said.

'You hop closer. It isn't glass. It won't break, and your blows don't seem to be being noticed on the other side.' Elton stood from his chair. 'I have to go down and ask John some questions.'

Simon didn't speak until Elton left the room. 'John's the sacrifice.'

'What?' Mia asked.

'He's the sacrifice,' Simon said matter-of-factly. 'Or we are. Whichever of us leaves the room first kills the other.'

'But we're tied and he's by the door,' I said. 'If he reaches for the door, we're dead. All three of us.'

'You're forgetting something,' Simon said.

'I hope it's three sets of wings.' I glanced down at the equipment list on my character sheet.

'No.' Mia set her finger to the last but one entry. 'This.'

'Oh.' I pushed back from the table.

'It's him or us. And there has to be a sacrifice.' Simon shook his head.

Mia drew her hand back. She had pointed to the scroll we took from the vampire. Power Word Kill. I could read the word from the parchment and John's warrior would die without ever knowing why. Without any chance.

Elton came back and took his seat. 'While you bang on the window, John's warrior glances around the room, then cautiously he reached for the door handle.'

'Do it!' Simon urged.

'I don't want to. It's wrong.' I pushed my character sheet away.

'It's three lost or one,' Simon said. 'Fineous whips the scroll case from Nicodemus's pack, knocks off the end cap, and shakes the scroll into the mage's hands.' He gave me a hard stare.

'I could do it if he had a chance. Any chance. If he could make a saving throw . . .'

'He can't,' Elton said. 'You say the word, he dies. That's how it works.'

'I won't.' This was about more than the game. It was about control. About losing control. Taking it back. Giving yourself a chance. 'I can't.'

Mia frowned. 'Nick—'

The door burst open and John rushed in.

'Out!' Elton roared, surging to his feet. 'You can't be in here—'

John pushed him back into his chair. 'This is serious. It's the hospital, Mia. Your mum. There's been a fire.'

CHAPTER 20

Simon's mum drove Mia and me to the Westminster Hospital where Mia's mother had been taken, blue-lighted from a fire at the Miller blocks.

I stopped asking questions early on. Mia hadn't been given much information and was giving out short answers. I didn't think an hour's snogging the previous night qualified me for giving comfort in such extreme circumstances. I was amazed that she even wanted me to come. Elton had volunteered and been rebuffed.

'I'm impressed they found you,' I said.

Mia narrowed her eyes at me. 'I let her know where I'll be. Put the number in her purse. She's not a bad mother. She cares. She just drinks a bit is all.'

'Sorry. I didn't mean—'

'It's OK. Just stop apologising.'

'S—' I caught myself and held my tongue. Sitting without speaking, I watched the lights go by as we drove through London's bleak midwinter.

Simon's mum dropped us off in the car park with best wishes, two thirds of a packet of digestive biscuits, and a bottle of lemonade. 'I'm sorry I can't stay, Mia. You've got money to get home? Yes? I hope she's better soon. Call if you need something. Nick, make sure she calls.'

The car behind started on the horn and we tumbled out to let Mrs Brett go.

Moments later, we were hurrying through the sliding doors into the A&E reception. When I'd escaped Ealing Hospital late on Thursday night, I'd hoped I was done with the NHS for a while, but here I was again under the too-bright lights, with the smell of antiseptic and desperation. I felt immediately nauseous and all my aches returned. I waited while Mia went to ask at the desk. I saw Eva three times, the top of her head, the side of her face, her eyes above the back of a bench. It wasn't her, of course. Just girls with the same dark, curly hair, but my imagination kept finding her. I blamed it on lack of sleep and a late-onset hangover.

'She's up on the ward. Come on.' Mia marched by and I followed.

'Burns ward?'

'General. Ward 31. Smoke inhalation.' Mia managed quite a pace and scorned the lifts in favour of the stairs. Despite my longer stride, I had trouble keeping up.

I waited in the corridor outside the ward while Mia went in. I walked the length of it several times to keep the ache from my legs. Somehow, standing still is harder than moving. A wheelchair stood abandoned in the ward entrance on my side of the doors. The temptation to sit down in it grew each time I passed by.

The fire had to be Rust's work. Under any other circumstances a fire at the home of an alcoholic chain smoker would explain itself. The woman drank herself insensible and her last cigarette ignited the bedclothes or armchair. But days after spilling Rust's blood, hard on the heels of him pouring flammable liquid through her letterbox . . . had to be him again.

It probably hurts to be an invalid at any age. At fifteen it crushes you. You go from feeling pretty much invincible to feeling useless.

Mia's mother had nearly been burned to death and tradition demanded that in my new role as maybe-boyfriend I step up and seek violent retribution on the two females' behalf. And yet Mia and her mum both seemed infinitely more capable of dealing with Rust than I did. And none of us had done very well last night.

I slumped into the wheelchair with a sigh of defeat and stared at the green wall before me. Demus must have known about the fire. Mia must mention it to me in the months and years to come, so wiping this week from my memory wouldn't wash the fact of it away. Did he try to stop it? Or did the mathematics of his quest demand that he let it happen? If he knew it had happened and now managed to stop it, then his chance to save 'his' Mia vanished as he jumped us all onto another timeline. So had he sat back coldly and let it happen? If the woman died it was on him. On me.

And what was Mia to him? An old flame? The love of his life? Mother to his children? Did he weigh that in the scales against the life of a middle-aged alcoholic? Was I that calculating?

Or perhaps the woman burned alive in her bed in his past and this time he had saved her from it at the cost of all his ambitions. I wasn't sure I wanted to know what he had done. But whatever he had done, it was hard to feel ownership of it.

When I was four I pushed my best friend down the stairs to claim a disputed toy. A blue metal-cast tractor, if I recall correctly. The fall had cost James Davis one of his baby teeth. It was eleven years ago and I couldn't manage to feel the slightest bit guilty about it. That small version of me had been a different person. His decisions made in a very different context, informed by experience that now had only fractional overlap with my own. And yet, the eleven years that stood between us was dwarfed by the twenty-five that separated me from Demus.

'She wants to see you.' Mia leaned through the swing doors to the ward and broke into my musings.

'Me?'

'Yes. You. Come on.' She vanished back through the doors.

I stood guiltily from the wheelchair and followed.

Just as Eva had been, Mia's mother was reduced by her hospital bed. She lay like a specimen on a dish, spoiling the pristine whiteness of the sheets with her thin, swarthy arms. She had a respirator over her face, which she took off to address me in a hoarse whisper.

'If my son were here, I wouldn't be talking to you, boy.'

'Yes, ma'am.' I nodded, aware that I was a poor substitute for her imprisoned gangland son.

'That boy. Weasel-face.' She replaced the oxygen mask and took a pained breath from it. 'That boy ain't right in the head.' She tapped her brow with a nicotine-stained finger. 'Got some screws loose.' She nodded.

I nodded too. It was true.

'They'll come after him for this. My lad's lot. He's going to wish he weren't born, that one.' Another painful drag on the mask. She coughed weakly and fought to stop it turning into something more. 'But till they catch hold of him.' She tilted her head toward Mia. 'She wants to lie low.' Dark eyes narrowed at me and any illusions I had that this was a polite request blew away in a cold wind. This was a mother wolf looking out for her cub. 'You keep her *safe*, Nick.'

'I will.' She knew my name! Mia had talked about me!

'OK.' A tired nod and a wave of her hand. I was dismissed.

'I'll come out in a bit.' Mia smiled at me, half-embarrassed, half-pleased.

She found me back in that wheelchair thirty minutes later.

'How is she?'

'Resting. The doctors seem more worried than she is. Well, according to the nurses. I didn't actually see any doctors . . . Anyway, smoke can mess you up. They have to watch her carefully, make sure she doesn't go downhill.'

'Sorry.'

'It's not your fault.' Mia's face hardened. 'We know who did it. And we know he isn't going to stop.'

I nodded. With most people, almost everyone, there's some level at which enough is enough. The level varies from one person to another, but there *is* a level. You didn't have to spend long in Rust's company to realise that he had no threshold. He would escalate any situation with startling rapidity to the point where he could count it as a victory, which meant the other party had to lose. His wasn't a personality built to last. At least, not in a society with laws and police to enforce them. But he would make quite a mess before he was finished. I was pretty sure of that!

'So, we lie low. Like your mum said. And wait for your brother's friends to sort it.' I tried to hide the hope from my voice.

Mia nodded, a touch unwillingly. 'If I see him, though . . .'

'Let's hope we don't.' I levered myself to my feet. 'Though, given that he knows where both of us live, it seems as if the option might be his rather than ours.'

'We could stay over at Elton's?' Mia said.

'They're like sardines in there already. John's got more room.'

Mia shook her head. 'I don't think I could be civil to his mum.'

'I know what you mean. His dad's a nice guy, though. He went round to the Arnots' to apologise for his wife and try to settle things. I mean, you can't. It's like trying to pick shit out of a sandwich. But at least he tried. Short of divorcing the woman, what can he do?'

'I guess. But I'm not staying there.'

'Simon's then. You heard Mrs Brett. She practically invited us, and they have a box room.' I'd stayed over at Simon's so many times I was starting to wear a me-shaped dent in the floor.

Mia nodded thoughtfully. 'Let's get some air first.'

The night had that bitter January edge to it that makes you so very glad we live in centrally heated houses and have warm beds to sleep in. I shivered at the thought that just a dozen generations ago, we'd have counted ourselves lucky to have mud and twigs between us and the outside, that we would have had to go out and labour in the frost, and huddle at night around a pile of burning sticks.

'Freezing.' I hugged myself. The orange glow of streetlights and the whiter illumination in the hospital car park both conspired to chase the darkness under the bushes, but any warmth they promised was a lie. Frost had started to trace its way across the cars, and the sounds of the street had taken on that brittle quality that cold brings.

'He could be watching, you know.' Mia stood close, her shoulder to my arm.

'What?'

'Rust. If he was after me, then he would only have to know which hospital they took Mum to. He must have known I would come to see her. So, all he had to do was wait out here and follow when I left.'

'Uh.' It had a certain uncomfortable ring of truth to it. It sounded like the sort of strategy a creature like Rust would use. Exploiting those bonds of human affection that he knew existed but didn't understand. 'Wouldn't he be more interested in your mother? She was the one that cut him after all . . . What did *you* do? You were a bit late paying a debt that was mostly fake anyway.'

'I crossed him. We both did. And we saw what Mum did to him. And last night just made it worse. He's the sort that keeps score.'

'He is.' I knew that much. Once he got a taste of you, Rust wasn't the sort to let go. Not even now, with Sacks's crew out hunting him. The interest he had in Mia had moved well past being financial. It may have been more than financial right from the start. And she'd told him no, seen him humiliated, twice. 'OK, what do we do?'

'Well, we don't go to Simon's. Not if we think Rust might be following.' Mia shook her head. Her breath plumed.

I sighed. Our options seemed to have been whittled down to a selection of unpleasant choices. 'Demus told me that once we have the chip he can make the "Rust problem" go away. He also reminded me that we need to get it done in the next few days, or the timing on the memory-wipe won't match with how it happened for him.'

'Easy then.' Mia didn't hesitate. 'We call the others and get this chip for Demus tonight. That way, we're all together if Rust comes and we're not anywhere where our families can get hurt.'

I bit my lip and nodded. We did need to get the thing done. And as much as I didn't like the idea of facing Rust out in the dark, I liked it more knowing my friends would be there and knowing he wouldn't be letting himself in through my back door in the small hours, walking upstairs toward Mother's room with a knife gleaming in his hand.

'Let's do it.'

CHAPTER 21

We called Elton first, from a piss-stinking phone box just down from the hospital. Mia stared out through the little graffitied panes of glass and held the door open against its leather hinges while I fumbled a ten-pence piece into the slot with numb fingers.

'Elton. We gotta do it tonight. No. Tonight. I'm not kidding. Yes. Yes, she should be fine. Smoke inhalation. She has to stay in. No. No. Yes. We'll call you from outside the Spot. About half an hour.' I put down the receiver. 'Said we'll meet him outside The Spotted Horse.' The pub was close to his flat.

I called John next. He bitched and moaned, of course, but in the end he said he'd come. I could hear the TV in the background and he sounded as if he was eating. 'I'll have to work on an excuse to get out, then call to say I'm staying over somewhere. Better to apologise after than to ask permission and be told no!'

'Great. Thanks, John.'

'Hey, tell future you to get me a hover board and we're all good. Catch you later. The Spot at eleven, right?'

'Right. See you—'

'Hey, wait. I forgot. How's Mia's mum?'

'Should be OK. Breathed in a lot of smoke. High tar.'

'Good. Good. And the lovely Mia?'

'She's coming with us.'

'Really?' A pause. 'Fine. She'll probably be more help than you, anyway.'

I hung up and dug in my pockets for another ten pence. 'Now for the difficult one . . .'

Mia offered me the necessary coin. 'I can sweet talk Simon, if you like?' She fluttered her eyelids in my direction. 'I think he likes me.'

'Simon?' I scoffed. 'He's less interested in girls than Elton is!'

Mia punched my arm. It hurt. 'You can be interested in girls without wanting to take them to bed. We're people, too, you know.'

'Sorry.' I rubbed my shoulder. 'Boys' school education. It's true. He likes you.' I handed her the phone.

She dialled the number and I took my turn at holding the door open, the extra cold being a price worth paying for fresher air.

The half of the conversation that I got to listen to didn't make much sense to me, but when she hung up after a far longer phone call than I had ever managed with Simon, Mia was grinning. 'He'll be there. He's telling his mum he's staying over at yours. I doubt she minds where he is, to be honest. She'll just be glad he's not in his room all evening.'

We walked back to the Miller blocks. I told Mia it was too far, but she said it was too cold to wait for buses. I think she was too agitated to stand still and wanted to be on the move. I relied on her for directions and we stuck to the high streets and the main roads, staying where it was well lit and well trafficked. If Rust was following us, he would be waiting for his moment. A dark alley, a lonely park. I was damned if I would just give it to him. I looked back a few times, but in London there's always someone following you by chance, so picking out someone doing it on purpose isn't exactly easy.

We crossed the Thames by Battersea Bridge, getting back south of the river where we belonged. The four great chimneys of the power station stood illuminated on the far bank, smokeless for the last couple of years now. A dinosaur on its back, legs in the air. I wondered what stood in the spot in Demus's time. Then it struck me.

'How's he going to get back?' I stopped dead centre of the bridge, the black waters of the Thames sliding beneath us, traffic roaring past a foot to our left.

'What? Who? And where?' Mia stopped a yard ahead and turned to face me.

'How will Demus get back to the future?'

Mia grinned. 'This really does sound like the film. You *have* to see it.'

'What does?'

'*Back to the Future*, silly. They need a lightning bolt to get back. It's the only way to get the power they need.'

I shook my head and gazed at the dead power station. 'There's not a lot of energy in a lightning bolt . . .' I nodded toward the chimneys. 'From what he said, that whole place over there couldn't do it, not if you ran it flat out. He'd need to drain the national grid.' I couldn't believe I hadn't thought of it earlier. How *was* he . . . I . . . going to get back?

Mia frowned. 'I guess he has it covered. He's a grown-up, after all. And it's not like he didn't have time to think this through.'

'You're not worried for him?' I felt slightly betrayed.

She shrugged. 'I don't know him. I guess I will, one day. I mean, I've only known you for just over a month. And thinking of Demus as you, well, that's difficult. It's great that he went through this effort to help me. But . . . you know . . . it's just really hard to think of any of it as real. It hasn't happened yet. And, whatever he says, I can't think of the future as set in stone. I can't wrap my head around that one. It would be like nothing we do matters . . . The most important thing here is that he says he can get Rust off our backs if we do this.'

'I guess . . .' My guaranteed recovery seemed important, too, but she was right, it was further in the future, less tangible.

'And even if he does somehow make Rust forget about me, I'm still not sure that breaking and entering is a clever move.'

'Maybe it's just the least dumb move?'

'Come on!' Mia shrugged and set off again. 'It's freezing up here.'

She was right again. The wind over the river cut through my coat as if it weren't even there. I bent my head, gritted my teeth against the ache in my bones, and followed her. I didn't know what Demus's escape plan was, but I found it hard to care too very much. He was old, unimaginably distant in time. I cared for him in the same vague way I had always cared for my future self, i.e. I made the occasional short-lived resolve to eat sensibly, I saved my pennies for the future in a high interest building society account, and I took the trouble to acquire useful qualifications. The rest had always been future-me's business and good luck to him.

We skirted by the Miller blocks, coming close enough to see the black stain above the windows of Mia's flat. It would be a long time before anyone lived in there again. The council would move them somewhere, but it might not be close.

'Bastard.' Mia muttered it under her breath.

'Could have been a lot worse.' It still could.

By the time we reached The Spotted Horse we were cold and tired and ready to quit. It looked inviting – the warm light through the puddle glass windows, the hubbub of conversation through the door – but I knew from experience that they wouldn't serve us in there. Not even a coke and a bag of crisps.

'I'll call Elton.' I nodded to a bank of phone boxes. The others should already be on their way.

'You realise this is seriously stupid?' Elton surprised us by coming down the high street rather than up it and stepping in between us, a hand on both our shoulders.

'We do,' I said. 'Mia's been trying to talk me out of it.'

'You don't believe this Demus guy anymore, Mia?' Elton sounded so grateful that I felt immediately sorry for him when Mia answered.

'I believe he's from the future, and I believe he's trying to help. I mean . . . if you had that power, to travel back and change things . . . There's so many ways you could help yourself. Why would you waste time doing what he's doing unless you meant it?'

'So what you trying to stop us for?' Elton asked, releasing our shoulders.

'Because of what you said,' Mia replied. 'This is seriously stupid. If we get caught we could get put in an institution. Nick, John, and Simon could get expelled from their posh school and miss out on university. Hell, if there's guard dogs, they might eat us. And for what? To make me better when I'm forty? I don't even want to be forty. Me? Forty years old? Whatever Demus says, I can't believe it's going to be like that. I could get hit by a bus tomorrow. I could. I don't care what he says about it.'

'I want you to be forty,' I said.

'I do, too,' Elton said. 'My parents are way past forty. There's still plenty of life to live. Don't give me this die young, stay pretty shit.' He reached into his pocket and drew out a crumpled bit of paper. 'Besides, there's this.' He offered it to Mia.

She straightened it out. The words were in my handwriting. The note Demus gave Elton in John's house. Mia paused to find her voice, then read it aloud. 'You marry him. Your friends and family come to the wedding.' Her eyes glistened. 'Who is "him"?'

'I've got an idea. But in the end it's not the important part,' Elton said. 'I want the future Demus has seen.'

'So . . . we're doing it then,' I said.

'Yup.' Elton nodded.

John and Simon arrived together about a quarter of an hour later. Just long enough of an extra wait in the freezing cold for us to start cursing them for chickening out.

'So, we all know what we're doing then?' I said, setting off up the street.

'No fucking idea.' Elton caught up with me. I tried to remember if I'd heard him swear before.

'Well,' John called after us. 'Not really. But I know where we're going, and it's not in that direction. We need the tube station.' And he headed off the opposite way.

It was a hike to Clapham South tube. I knew I'd overdone it. I doubted I'd be able to get out of bed the next day. But at least the pace kept me warm. Warmish. Warmer than I would have been standing still. We stopped once while I was sick into someone's garden hedge.

At the station we dug in our pockets for the required fare.

'It doesn't seem right, having to pay for the privilege of committing a crime.' John poked through his change. 'Really, we should jump the barriers.'

We paid for our tickets, though, like upstanding members of society, and went to stand on the musty platform.

The train was crowded with the people who would be our competition when it came to escaping the city centre in the small hours of the night. The tube trains ran late enough to fill up London's nightclubs and theatres, then inexplicably closed down before anyone wanted to come home. Since we didn't have a getaway car, I'd made sure we had enough cash on us for the extortionate return by taxi.

It was a straight shot from Clapham South to Old Street, eleven stops on the Northern Line, back across the Thames. For the best part of an hour we rattled through the subterranean night, passing beneath the river and the heart of the city. We used the time trying to firm up the very loose plan we'd already come up with, shouting over the clatter of the train. John had given us a rough layout of the place and secured the computer passwords from his father. Simon had been hitting his dad's books, sharpening the edge of his talent for rooting stuff out of computer files without permission. To my knowledge, Elton had never broken a law in his life, but he could climb like a gecko, and from his dad's stories about keeping bad guys out of buildings, he knew a few things about how to get into them. Mia and I were hopefully just going to be interested observers. We could keep watch or something . . .

'We're probably just going to fail to get in and end up coming home again,' Simon said.

Nobody disagreed with him.

I sat beside Mia and our hands found each other in the gap between us. I tried not to hold on too tight. We clattered through one station then the next, spitting out a few passengers, squeezing in three times as many. I watched our reflection warped by the curving double layer of the carriage window. Our images hung ghostly above the advertisements as they slid by, cigarettes, lingerie, cars, then darkness. I tried to think of us not only on steel tracks thundering inevitably on into the inky tunnel, but on equally un-jumpable tracks carrying us forward into a future just as certainly at a steady sixty minutes an hour whether we liked it or not.

Just before Christmas, as light relief, our English master had set us the task of writing an essay in which we described what advice we would have to offer ourselves if we could go back to when we first entered Maylert aged eleven. Or, if we were feeling more imaginative, what advice our future selves might offer us right now if they could step back from the end of our, hopefully, long and illustrious careers.

I had written something worthy about paying more attention in class then lightened it with some tips on buying shares in Atari. But, right now, it seemed that Mr Arnot's direction to 'kiss the girl' was pretty sound advice. Certainly Demus didn't seem to have discovered anything in the following decades that he felt important enough to pass on.

'We're here.' John tapped my shoulder. I'd been dozing.

'Sorry.' I got up after Mia, swaying with the motion of the carriage and reaching for the hanging supports to keep my feet.

We pushed out onto the platform, then up the escalators until the station regurgitated us back into the cold.

'Come on, it's this way.' John glanced at his *A to Z* and led off.

'You sure you been here before?' Elton asked.

'Once. Months ago. And I really wasn't paying much attention.'

John took us away from the late-night bustle of pubs and wine bars around the station down darker and lonelier streets. If we were in the suburbs, they would have called the area he navigated us into an industrial estate, but inner London has too much history and too little space for such contrivance. I guessed that the looming structures around us had once been Victorian factories where children dodged in and out of steam-driven engines while trying to keep all their fingers attached. Now most of them were probably fashion houses or design studios. We passed a grim doorway to a building that looked as if it might have once been an abattoir. The sign said 'Dance Studio 44'.

'Here.' John stopped where the wall of the previous building gave way to a high wire fence with a thick hedge behind it. Ahead of us a driveway led in, sealed by a drop bar. A darkened reception hut stood a few yards back.

'Doesn't look like a laboratory to me,' Elton said as we walked past.

'What are laboratories supposed to look like?' Mia asked.

'The sign says Motorola.' Simon pointed.

'It looks like an office building,' Elton said.

'That's pretty much what labs are,' I said. 'It's not all boiling cauldrons and Frankenstein machines. Besides, did you notice the chimneys?' A number of long thin pipes led up into the air from the top of the rear wall. 'That's a lab. The chimneys vent the fumes from fabrication with semi-conductors.'

'What he said.' John nodded. 'It rings a bell now Nick mentions it.'

John turned around and led us back up the deserted street, toward the main entrance. A lone man walked by on the other side of the road, head down, focused on his own business.

John paused at the entry. 'The primary defence seems to be a metal bar across the access road, approximately . . . hmmm . . . three feet off the ground. Elton, as our all-star athlete, do you think you can get past it?'

'Come on.' Elton ignored John and led us all in along the narrow path between the gate and the admissions block. We came into a car park before the main building, an empty expanse of tarmac lit by sporadic lampposts.

We gathered in a dark corner out of sight from the street. Elton shouldered the sports bag he'd brought with him. The contents clanked and appeared to be heavy. 'This place will be alarmed. Our best bet is for me to check out the fire escapes and see if any of the doors can be opened from the outside. If that doesn't work, I can go up on the roof and see if there's a way in through the access door or a skylight. Often they don't bother to alarm inaccessible entrances.' He looked around.

'If the police come, or a security guard shows up, then leg it through those bushes at the back, get clear, then start walking. Deny everything.'

We stood shivering with anticipation, but mainly with the cold, while Elton headed off to the fire escapes. His only real qualification for the job was a healthy body. If it came to scrambling from the top of the fire escape to the roof Elton was a hundred times better situated to doing it than Simon, fifty times better than me in my current condition, and at least ten times as able as John or Mia.

After five or ten minutes fiddling about with the fire doors on the first and second floor, Elton shimmied up onto the railing, grabbed hold of the edge of the roof and vanished over. We caught a last glimpse of his legs waving and he was gone.

'He won't get in,' Simon said.

'Not without a hammer at least.' John nodded. 'And surely the alarms will go off whatever he does? I mean, at our house the alarm goes off if you sneeze after midnight. And this place has to have more to protect it than something my father had installed at home?'

'Just be ready to run,' Mia said. 'It takes ages for police to answer an alarm. If we hear one and leave immediately then we should be fine.'

'What if it's a silent alarm?' Simon muttered.

'Silent alarms are for when you want to catch someone.' I was making it up as I spoke, but it sounded right. 'In a place like this, you want whoever it is to leave as soon as possible. The quicker they're out, the less damage they do. Vandals could do thousands of pounds worth of damage in a place like this, and some random teens aren't going to be able to pay it back. Best to have a noisy alarm and scare them off. I think.' Despite my argument, none of them looked convinced. I tried a different tack. 'Look, the fact is that Demus remembers "waking up" in a park a few days from now, missing any memory of the last two weeks. To me, that says we get in and get the chip. So whether it's blind luck or skill, or mixture of the two, I think this is going to work. How else—'

'Maybe I cause the memory loss by hitting you over the head with a hammer?' Mia suggested.

A flash of a light at the top landing of the fire escape caught my eye. 'Is that . . . ?'

'It's Elton with a torch.' Mia started forward.

Against all the odds Elton was leaning out from the fire door, beckoning us.

I took a moment to hide the bag with Demus's headbands in the bushes to collect later, then set off after Mia, with John and Simon at my heels. 'If I built a lab I'd wire it so that the alarm went off if the fire doors were opened after office hours.'

'Perhaps he disabled it,' John said.

'This is Elton we're talking about, not a cat burglar. I don't think he's ever swiped as much as a chocolate bar from a corner shop.'

We climbed up, our shoes startlingly loud on the cold metal steps. 'You got in, then.' I stated the obvious.

'Catch on a skylight was gone. No alarms up there. Dropped down on to a posh desk. Probably John's dad's.' Elton shrugged. 'You sure they're keeping this super seekret chip here? It all seems a bit easy.'

'Let's find out.' Mia squeezed past him and the rest of us followed.

Nobody had thought to bring a torch except for Elton. Fortunately, he'd thought to bring five. Though two of them were the front lights off his brothers' bikes.

'Take us to the mainframe,' I hissed.

'Why are you talking like that?' John asked in a normal voice.

'Uh . . . security guards?'

'Fair point,' he hissed back. 'Though if they have any, we're fucked.'

'Place this size might have one or two,' Elton said. 'None, if we're really lucky. Anyway, let's hope they're in their room watching TV and having a cup of tea. Keep your torch use to a minimum, though. If they do a patrol, they'll have torches of their own and you'll see them coming.'

'Mainframe,' I prompted.

'Well, Dad did show me a room full of computers . . . or computer. On the middle floor, I think.' John reached a crossing of corridors and turned slowly. 'Let me get my bearings. It's a pretty big place.'

Simon kept very close behind me, breathing heavily, far more heavily than the climb up the fire escape should merit.

'You OK, Si?'

'Great.' He shone his light both ways down the intersecting corridor. 'Just waiting for the guard dogs.'

'This way.' John led us off again.

Right up to the very last minute, John gave a great impression of being lost. I was about to helpfully berate him as he stood halfway down a nondescript corridor on the first floor, staring at his fingers, but he beat me to it.

'Here.' He turned and patted the door behind him.

'You're sure?' Unlike the hospital, Motorola seemed dead set against signs of any kind other than the names of the office occupants, set in tiny letters on plastic cards slid into holders on various doors.

'It's in there.' John stood back.

Elton tried the door. 'Locked.' He took a crowbar from his bag. 'So far, we've just been trespassing. Now, we're breaking and entering. That's what the charge will be. And if we come out with something that's not ours, that's burglary. Just so we're clear.'

We all nodded, the torchlight managing to make us look like proper criminals. Elton shrugged and set to work. The frame splintered and the door opened without further protest. He reached in and flicked on the lights. We were in the middle of the building with no windows, so no worry about being seen from the outside.

The computers were something of a disappointment. I had been conditioned by years of television to expect something out of James Bond or *Thunderbirds*. The industrious spooling back and forth of reels of magnetic tape while banks of lights lit fitfully, hinting at great works of computation. Instead, we were presented with several uninspiring grey boxes about the size of refrigerators, humming gently to themselves. A table at the back of the room sported several monitors, each with a built-in keyboard.

John handed over the piece of paper bearing the passwords he had copied from his father's list, and Simon set to his task. The first worrying thing was quite how slowly Simon worked what would hopefully be his magic. He typed at a rate of about three letters per minute, hovering one finger over the keyboard in a seemingly endless search for whatever character he wanted. The result appeared before him in glowing green on the grey screen. It took him forever to get through the passwords.

'They don't work,' he said.

'How can they not work?' I asked.

'Like this.' He hit the return button. The legend 'password or username incorrect' appeared.

Simon tapped the word at the top of the list. 'This is obviously his username . . . all lowercase, though . . .' He turned to look at John. 'There weren't any capital letters in any of these passwords?'

'I . . . There might have been . . . Is that important then?' John looked sheepish.

'Yes.' Simon squeezed a considerable amount of passion into one short word.

'Can't you try them again and use capitals this time?' Mia asked.

'I can.' Simon exhaled a long sigh. 'There are quite a few possible combinations.'

'How long?' I asked. Simon knew exactly how many combinations there were.

'That depends on how stupidly the passwords were chosen.' He started typing. Slowly. 'And if I get in, then I have to hunt around, and if we're really, really lucky, I might get the combinations to one or more safes, and our chip might be in one of them. So if we want to be out of here before morning, then you lot had better start looking for the safe we need.'

He had a point.

'It would be quicker if we split up to search,' John said.

'You realise that you sound like the doomed teenager in every horror film ever?' Elton asked.

John and Elton both had points.

'We're not in a horror film.' I tried to sound confident. 'And this is a big building. We should split up and go find this safe. Let's hope there's just one of the buggers.'

I turned back toward the door. Someone had hung a whiteboard on the back of it, and written on the board in red marker pen was the legend 'Tower of Tricks'.

'What the fuck?' I stood, staring at it. Something about the lettering seemed familiar. 'This is straight from our D&D game! Did one of you just write this here?'

John came to stand at my shoulder, a chorus of nos following him. 'Not me. Stupid name for the place anyway. It's not a tower. The whole building is only three storeys.'

Against all my instincts for self-preservation, I found myself alone in a cold, dark building with a bicycle lamp to light my way, rooting through deserted offices and empty labs, hunting for a safe that I wasn't sure I would recognise even if I found it.

I had wanted to team up with Mia, but couldn't think of a way to say so without it being taken as insulting her ability to play an equal role . . . or painting myself as incapable. And so here I was. Creeping through each room as if that might stop the boogieman from noticing me.

I had the top floor to search. Elton had the middle floor where Simon was working. John and Mia each had half of the bottom floor. He said he thought there was a better chance of the safe being down there. It held the more senior offices, and some administration rooms.

There's something about the way a handheld light throws the shadows around that quickly convinces your mind that everything in the room is focused on you. Waiting for its chance to strike, scurrying away as the light swings toward it. I found myself turning on the spot, faster and faster, trying to catch whatever it was that was stalking me before it pounced.

I forced myself to stop and to carry on the search, heart pounding, ready to jump at every shadow. In films they had wall safes hidden behind large portraits. The offices at the laboratory were singularly lacking in large portraits. In fact, they seemed to have a rule against posters or pictures of any kind. One of the larger offices had a number of framed certificates hanging behind the desk. No wall safe behind them, though.

I entered another room. A workshop of some sort, with towering shelves filled with slide-out plastic bins each brimming with electronic components. I walked in, footsteps too loud, breath pluming even in here. The swing of my lamp revealed a figure standing silent in the darkness at the end of the first aisle. I froze, stopped breathing, and clenched the lamp so tight I managed to turn it off briefly.

'Stay back! I've got . . . a . . .' Got a what? A knife? A gun? A pointy stick? I snatched a Stanley knife from the shelf behind me.

The figure remained unmoving. Terrified, I edged toward it. 'Who . . . what?'

A white lab coat hung on a coat stand. Mocking me. The figure that my imagination had constructed fell apart. I stood feeling foolish and relieved, trying to calm my heart. They wouldn't keep an important safe in a storeroom. I put the knife in my pocket and backed out, keeping one eye on the coat stand and its ghostly occupant.

My hunt had led me back almost to the fire door we had entered by. I could feel the draught from the fire escape as I went to check the last door on the corridor. I hugged myself against the cold. Elton had left a screwdriver to keep the door open a fraction, just in case. Somehow it felt better that it not close on us. Now I noticed a dark object just before the door. A bag? Something not much bigger than a football. I moved closer, directing the weakening beam of my light toward it. A plastic carrier bag? Two bags. One full of something, the other mostly empty . . . I tilted my head to the side, trying to make sense of it, and stepped closer.

'I wouldn't.'

I squealed like a little girl at the sound of the unexpected voice behind me.

'Steady. It's only me.'

'Jesus, fuck!' I clutched my chest. Demus stood behind me, hands raised. In the lamplight he looked half dead, white skinned, dark circles about his eyes.

'What the hell are you doing here?'

'Helping,' he said. 'I arrived before you and disabled the alarms from the outside.'

'If you were going to come here anyway, what do you need us for?' I felt both angry and relieved.

'Passwords, combinations, athletic ability. All that sort of thing.' He shrugged. 'Besides, from what I gathered about it after the event, you were all here. So I needed you to be here.'

I frowned, trying to find a flaw in his logic. My logic. 'What's in the bags?'

'Sacks,' he said.

'Bags,' I repeated, and flashed my light back toward them. 'Tesco bags, by the look of them.'

'Sacks,' Demus said again. 'And you really shouldn't look.'

'You're not making any sense.' The contents of the fuller bag looked wet.

'Sacks is in the bag. Well, his head is. The other one has a hammer in it and a hacksaw. Rust left them there on his way in.'

CHAPTER 22

'That psycho's in the building?' I started back in.

'Woah.' Demus grabbed my arm. It felt weird holding myself back like that. 'Where do you think you're going?'

'To stop him!' I tried to shake off Demus's grip. 'Mia's on her own in there. And the others.'

Demus held on, his fingers biting painfully into my bicep. 'This is what happens. Mia survives.'

'What?' I shook my head. 'You said you don't remember this. I'm supposed to wipe my memory.'

'I don't remember it happening, but I remember the aftermath. I've lived with it for more than half my life. I never asked about it, but some facts can't be avoided.'

'The aftermath?' I tried to haul myself free, but he hung on grimly, as strong as I was, or as weak.

'This is the Tower of Tricks. There's no escape without sacrifice.' Demus released me with what sounded like a cry of pain and slumped back against the wall. 'There's a price to pay.'

'Tell me what you know!' I shouted it at him.

'I know that this way you can bring Mia back. Return her past to her and give her a future. I know that one day, that will mean more to you than everything. Anything.'

'At what cost?' I grabbed him, taking the front of his coat in two handfuls. 'At what cost?' The bike lamp fell to the floor, shadows spinning crazily.

'You lose friends here, Nick. I lose friends. And I've had twenty-five years to mourn that fact. There's blood on my hands. Whatever I do, there's blood on my hands.'

'Who? Who do I lose?' I slammed him back against the wall.

'Does—' He coughed. Something dark stained his lips. 'Does it matter? Would . . . Would it change what you do?'

'I . . .' I tried to think of losing any of them. Of the look on Simon's mother's face on learning that her only son was dead. Of the Arnots, if they lost Elton. 'No! I'm not losing any of them. Tell me how to stop it!'

'You can't stop it. It's the sacrifice. It's what she costs us. Her life saved. Others lost. One or many? Elton set you the puzzle already. And you ran from it. Ask me again how to stop it and I might tell you. But then you'd have to decide. I could tell you where to find Rust. One word. One word.'

'I . . .' Like the spell. One word, and someone who would have lived, dies.

'Or let it play out. As it already *has* played out. Let my past be your future. And save Mia.'

'Mia.' One short word that sent a hundred vivid images flooding through my mind's eye. I wanted her. More than anything. More, in that moment, even than I wanted to be well. I stood back, releasing Demus.

He straightened, wincing. He had blood around his mouth. In the light and shadow from the fallen lamp he looked demonic, almost the vampire he had once seemed.

'I don't know what you do, Nick. I don't remember this conversation. I remember the next week. I remember the shit I had to deal with. The bodies that needed to go into the ground. None of this is good. None of it can be. But it happened.'

'I can't play this game. I'm sorry.' I stepped away, bent, and picked up the light. 'I need to unstick the future, jump us onto another time-line. We all need a chance. I can't walk your path. I'm sorry.' I glanced down the dark corridor. 'Your Mia is old. Forty. She's lived a life . . .'

Demus bowed his head. 'How easily the young sacrifice the old. When you get to forty, it won't seem quite so clear-cut. Believe me. But . . . Well, just remember that you told me the old were a price worth paying.'

'I didn't say that.' Not exactly. Though I kind of had.

Demus pulled back his right sleeve. 'I don't have a scar here.' He drew a finger across the back of his wrist.

'What?' I wondered if he had gone mad or was just trying to dis-tract me while Rust killed my friends.

'I don't have a scar here.' He shrugged. 'If you did . . . then you couldn't be me. Could you?' He covered his wrist with his sleeve again. 'I remember that three people die here tonight. Do it your way and maybe it will be more. Maybe fewer.' He met my gaze, narrowing his eyes against the light. 'It's in your pocket.'

I reached into my coat pocket and there it was, the Stanley knife. I took it out and set the small, razor-sharp blade to the back of my other wrist.

'Think about it.' Demus didn't plead. I was grateful for that.

'No time.' And I drew the blade across my skin. I didn't press hard, but the blood came quickly, along with a sharp, sick-making pain. I turned away, retching. I would have a scar where Demus didn't. He wasn't me. His past was no longer my future.

'Restaurant.'

'Huh?' I turned back, wiping acid vomit from my mouth.

'That's the killing word. That's where you'll find Rust and remake the future.'

John had mentioned a staff restaurant down on the ground floor. I started off. 'You coming?'

'Why should I?' Demus called after me. 'It's not my future anymore.'

I reached the corner and looked back. 'It still matters!'

'To you maybe.' His voice came from the dark, further back than my dying torch could show. Silence. Then, just as I was about to go, 'That was the solution to your other problem, too, you know.'

'What? What was?'

'In the Tower of Tricks. Someone had to die. You should have used Power Word Kill on the old man. Everything would have gone away. One old man dead.'

'Come on!' And I was running for the stairwell. Only silence followed.

I reached the first floor before nerves started to set in. I was hunting a deranged killer in a darkened building. On my own. Rust had somehow managed to murder and decapitate a well-known local gang leader and then trail us across London carrying the man's head in a shopping bag. My plan appeared to centre on confronting him with my trusty Stanley knife whose blade, although proven to be sharp, stood less than an inch long.

I leaned out into the corridor from the stairwell and hollered. 'Elton! Simon!' I drew breath for another shout when, against all the odds, two lights appeared at the far end of the corridor and came swinging crazily toward me.

'We got it! We got it!' Elton was in the lead, holding a flat black box above his head, any concern that too much noise might bring a security guard clearly forgotten.

'We got it!' Simon came puffing behind him, red-faced.

'Got what?' I glanced around for Rust.

'The chip, doofus!' Elton bounced up to me. 'Si got the combination. I found the safe. A big thing like from World War II, just standing in the corner of an office.'

'We gotta go. Rust's here. He's killed Sacks and I think he's after Mia.'

'Rust?' Elton blinked and took a step back. 'The lunatic who torched Mia's place? What's he doing here?'

'Murdering people. He followed us. Come on.' I started down the stairs, feet flying. 'We have to get the others and go.'

We emerged onto the ground floor, finding it dark and silent.

'John! Mia!' I yelled. It had worked before.

Nothing.

'You guys go that way. I'll go this way.' I had spotted a sign to the restaurant.

'You're kidding, right?' Elton grabbed my shoulder. 'You said he killed Sacks? And you want to split up again?' He let go and pulled the crowbar from his bag. 'We take this sucker out together.'

'John took one half of this floor. Mia took the other. We need to get them both. Go! I got this!' I waved my little knife as fiercely as I could. Simon and Elton weren't dying on my watch. I'd get to the restaurant alone.

'No way—'

A distant cry cut Elton off, coming from the direction I'd tried to send them.

'Come on!' And hefting his crowbar he took off, Simon lumbering dutifully behind.

I pretended to run with them, then turned sharply and ran the other way.

The lights were on at the front of the restaurant. I pushed the doors open with shaking hands, trying not to let them squeak. The food counter stood before me, all closed up and covered. Tables and chairs stretched away into the shadows toward darkened windows. A little way ahead of me a figure lay face down in his own blood. A black guy in uniform. A security guard sprawled on the tiles, a gleaming red puddle forming around his side.

Further back into the room something rattled, and I raised the feeble beam of my bicycle lamp.

Rust sat at one of the tables close to the windows, Mia in the chair in front of him. The blade he had was literally a hundred times bigger than mine, a full-sized machete, the bloody cutting edge held within inches of Mia's neck.

'Little. Nicky. Hayes.' Rust put a cigarette in the corner of his mouth. 'Come to play?'

'You're mad.' I couldn't help but state the obvious.

Rust shrugged. 'If I kill all the witnesses, what has anyone got on me but rumours?' He turned his blade. The blood looked black, like oil. 'People say I don't know where to stop. I say, if you never stop, they'll never catch you.'

Mia stared at me, eyes pleading. I would be doing the same thing in her place. I had no idea what to do. He could cut her throat with a motion and kill me almost as easily. At every moment there were endless worlds branching away from us, worlds where Mia lay dying, worlds where she somehow elbowed him in the face and broke free, and through it all I was stuck in this one, where I stood like an idiot with no plan and less hope. Demus had been right. I could have saved her. He knew she survived. And somehow, by rushing down here to play the hero, I'd let her die.

'We've been waiting for you to show up, Nick.' Rust kept his voice conversational. 'I wanted you to see her die.'

'Don't. You don't have to do this!' I stepped forward.

'You mistake me.' Rust moved the blade closer to Mia's neck. 'I *want* to do it.'

185

'Just don't.' I took another step. Five yards and half a dozen chairs separated us.

'You've got a choice, Nick. You can go back and turn on the main lights so you get a better view. That way, she gets to live sixty seconds longer. Or you can say no, and I'll do it now.'

'I . . .' Movement in the darkness. Someone was advancing from behind them. There must be a back way in. 'Wait! I'll do it.'

I started to back toward the light switches by the entrance as slowly as I could.

'Quicker!' Rust pressed the flat of the machete blade to Mia's throat, the cutting edge just beneath her chin. She cried out in terror. 'Mia's dying for you to see her better.'

Chairs squealed across the floor as I pushed them aside, hoping to cover the sounds of the approach behind them. I reached the switches and set my hand against them. 'Lower the blade.'

The figure was behind them now, one hand raised and grasping what might have been a fire extinguisher.

'Really? You're trying to give me order—'

Rust's sneer was cut off as the object struck his head. I flicked all the switches and squinted against the sudden glare, staggering forward, tripping over everything in my path.

Blinking away afterimages and a sudden blurriness, I could make out Mia on the floor, supporting herself on one arm, the other hand clutching her crimson neck. Rust and his attacker were locked together on the floor, rolling, chairs tumbling around them. I fought off a moment's disorientation. An unexpected sweetness filled my mouth, and either a distant alarm had gone off or my ears were ringing.

I pulled myself together and rushed in to grab Rust's arms, trying to haul him off the other guy. Somehow, with a strength I hadn't thought I owned, I managed it. As I pulled him clear of Demus, my older self swung his arm. He had hold of a hammer and the crunch it made against the side of Rust's forehead was like nothing I'd ever heard or ever wanted to hear again. Rust went limp in my arms and fell bonelessly when I dropped him a moment later.

'Mia?' I turned toward her.

'I'm OK.' She took her hand from her neck, her fingers red. 'I think . . .'

It looked to be a shallow cut. Blood wasn't flooding down her neck or anything.

'You'll have a . . . lovely scar.' Demus coughed. More blood ran from his mouth than came from Mia's neck.

'Are you . . . OK?' I asked. He didn't look OK.

'Three people die here tonight.' Demus lowered his gaze and mine followed it to the hilt of Rust's machete, jutting from beneath Demus's ribs. 'Like I said.'

'Shit. Look, don't move. I'm calling an ambulance!'

He caught my wrist. 'Don't. It's not you that calls them.'

I tried to pull free. 'Enough with that! I changed things. Remember? This isn't your time anymore. I'm not even you.' I showed him my left wrist, sticky with blood from my self-inflicted cut.

'Wait!' Mia lurched to her feet. 'All this was for nothing then . . . ?'

Demus ignored her. He reached forward with his other hand, wincing as the machete shifted. He pushed his left hand forward exposing the wrist and a faint white seam of scar. 'You can always fool yourself, Nick. I showed you my right wrist before. You cut your left one. It's the natural way to do it. Three people will die here. Just like I remember.'

'But . . . you said I'd lose a friend.'

Demus nodded toward the body lying by the serving area. A pang of regret crossed his brow. 'Jean Arnot. You said you were prepared to sacrifice someone "old" for someone young. Elton never forgives you for it. I'm sorry. You lose a friend. It's silly. We were just kids, and I haven't seen him for longer than you've been alive . . . but I still miss him.'

'I don't understand.' Mia turned toward the body by the door as if only now noticing it. She looked lost.

I didn't want to understand, but I started to. John's father had been to see Elton's dad to apologise for his wife's behaviour. Mr Arnot did agency work as a security guard. John's father had a laboratory that must sometimes need guards to fill gaps in the rota. Cruel chance had done the rest.

Mia started to walk toward the body, stopped and crossed to us.

'Mia . . .' Demus blinked away sudden tears. He lifted a hand to the hilt jutting from his side. His voice fell lower still. 'I can't speak to her. But you will, Nick. You'll understand.'

'You never did have a plan to go back,' I said.

'No.' A whisper. The blood was spreading underneath him. I was watching myself die.

'You need to be in hospital . . .'

A shake of the head. I had to lean in to hear him now. 'The two of you have to erase today from your minds, Nick. It's important. You can't know these things. They'll poison you both.'

'But . . . I *die* here?' Suddenly forty didn't seem so old.

'I knew this was the end for me, but I didn't know how. I'm not brave enough to have done it knowing all the details, and to let it happen just as you saw it. Rub those memories out.'

'Christ.' Mia knelt beside me. 'Nick? You came back to do *this* . . . for me?' She looked at Demus as if truly seeing him as me for the first time. 'You came here to die for *me*?'

He coughed and looked away. 'Maybe my cancer returned. Maybe I found out after I came back that time travel may only work on living things, but they don't live long afterward. It's not a gentle process. The truth is that neither of you should know what I gave up or why. Neither of you want to know.' He lay back, breath rasping through bloody lips, growing fainter with each cycle. It's an odd thing to watch yourself die. It filled me with a dozen different feelings, none of which I have names for. His breathing grew so shallow that I thought he had gone, but Demus sucked in a deeper breath. 'I've given you what you need. Take away the memories. Give yourself back your future. Live your lives.'

CHAPTER 23

We didn't tell the others about Mr Arnot, or Demus, or Rust. Mia and I ran from the restaurant when Demus shuddered out his last breath. We found the others hurrying toward us down the corridor and we herded them back, leaving by the ground floor fire exit. Somehow, I had the presence of mind to retrieve the bag with Demus's two headbands from the car park bushes, and then we walked, rather than ran, back toward the tube station and the taxi rank outside it.

None of us spoke much. Mia and I didn't speak at all. My coat hid the bloodstains on my jumper. The great majority of the blood on Mia's neck had come off the machete blade, and she wiped it away before anyone saw it. How much trouble we were in depended entirely on Elton. We were either free and clear, with the blame squarely at the feet of Rust and a mysterious man with no identity, or we were in over our heads with an endless and unanswerable mountain of questions and accusations to face.

Elton held his tongue. When they told him that his father was dead, and where he died, and when and how, he said nothing. He said nothing about it afterwards either. Not to me. Ever. He knew Demus would have known, but he never asked how much the man had told me. And although I could have told him that I hadn't known his father was there, and I had done my best to save everyone, and that in the end I had given my life for it . . . the fact remained that Demus had known Jean Arnot would die there. And the fact remained that Demus gave his all to keep us as his own past, so that what he asked me to do would matter to the future of his Mia. And the chances were that a quarter of a century from now I would return to 1986, not knowing the details of that night in the laboratory, but being sure of two things. First, that I was prepared for three people who walked into that building not to walk out of it again. And second, that one of them would be me.

I met Mia in Richmond Park two days later. She called me to arrange it. It was further for her to come than for me, but she knew I wasn't well and she said she could walk from her crazy aunt's. It was cold and grey and threatening rain, but somehow neither of us wanted to be indoors. It felt too claustrophobic, what with the space that the guilt and unspoken accusations would take up.

She was waiting for me, the bench to either side of her still frosty. She'd come without makeup, and without hairspray her hair looked so different that for a moment I wasn't sure who was sitting there.

'How is he?' I put the plastic bag with its heavy contents between us.

'Angry,' she said. 'Sad. All the things you would expect.'

'And you?'

'The same.' She pressed her lips into a bitter line. 'You should have told me who Demus was from the very start. How much damage all of this would cause. I didn't want any of it.'

'I should have told you who he was as soon as I knew,' I agreed. 'The rest I didn't know.' I raised a hand in defence. 'I know now. I *will* know when I come back . . . If I do. If me and Demus really are the same person, exactly. But that's a loop I can't get my head around right now.' I patted the bag. 'I'm going to take away the last couple of weeks. Rub out the memory of it all.'

'Why?' The stare she gave me was all suspicion. 'That's what he wanted you to do.'

I took out one of the headbands. 'Mr Arnot is dead. I can't bring him back. Nobody can. Demus gave his life to stop Rust taking yours. And Rust is dead. And that's a good thing. I can't feel sorry about that. So, if I don't do what Demus asked me to . . . If I don't do the last thing that I asked myself to do . . . then what would it all achieve?' I drew a long breath. If things didn't go how Demus remembered, then I wasn't Demus. If I wasn't Demus, then my chances of surviving leukaemia stopped being guaranteed and became statistically unlikely. If I said that to Mia, though, what kind of pressure would that lay on her? She had the power to save me, but asking her to do it was beyond me. 'All I can see is that if I don't blank these weeks just like he remembers doing, then it would mean that none of this was for anything. That you could still get hurt years from now and that I'd missed the chance to help someone I gave my life to save.'

'I never asked—'

'I know you didn't.'

'I don't want you to come back and do this.'

'I don't want to either. And the way I see it, I don't need to. We can record your memories and use them to restore you if you really do have this accident. Who's going to make me come back at that point?'

'Good. Don't come back. Don't be him ever.'

'I won't.' It wasn't true, though. If I didn't come back how would the memories work? How would any of it work? Still, I didn't want to come back. I didn't intend to. You would have to love someone a ridiculous amount to do that.

'Promise?' She met my gaze, serious.

'I have no intention of coming back so Rust can stick a machete through me,' I said. 'And I'm not trying to make you feel guilty over any of this. If you use the headband to erase the last two weeks like I'm about to do, then neither of us will even know what really happened in that laboratory. And I think that Demus was right about that being a good thing.'

'So, you know how to work this gadget?' She peered at it over her nose and for a moment the old Mia was back, the Mia from the D&D table considering one of Elton's death traps.

'I do.' I had installed the stolen chip and read the manual. 'And I've written a short catch up for me to read when it's done. I just need you to make me read it and to keep me from freaking out. Because as far as I will know, I'll have just jumped forward in time from whenever my most recent memory was. And I may be a bit surprised to find myself suddenly sitting here with you.'

Mia suppressed a smile. 'When will you set it for?'

'I'm aiming for just after I knocked Devis over outside your door and we chased him off. That way it will fit with when Demus's memories stopped.'

'You'll miss out on some good moments as well as some bad ones,' Mia said.

'I will.' I met her gaze. 'I'll have to learn to dance again.' I was thinking of her kisses, though. I would miss that memory. But also, I wouldn't have to remember watching myself die, and Demus wouldn't have to enter that building knowing how things would play out. It must be hard knowing you're about to die. But to have to do it to a script. To step into the blow you know is coming. That was too much to ask of anyone. Or myself.

I put the headband on, feeling rather self-conscious, though apart from an old woman in the distance walking her dog there was nobody around. In one hand I held the pocket calculator that interfaced to the band via a lead. In the other, the notes I had made for myself.

The skeleton of what had happened since Demus picked us up in his BMW outside the Miller blocks. Enough to bridge the gap, but avoiding detail. I finished with strict instructions not to ask too many questions or pursue the matter further. I had time travel to invent. Not to mention the headbands themselves.

'Look. I've done the same thing for you. You can choose how far you want to go back. Just enter the date like this and hit equals.' I showed her the display on my calculator then got out the other headband. 'I've written notes for you, too, though you should write the last page yourself, so you believe it.'

Mia took the notebook and the offered pen. She blew into her hands and began to write. 'It's a bit like writing a character sheet. You know, for D&D. I could tell myself anything. Make a new Mia maybe.'

'I rather like the old one,' I said.

She glanced at me and smiled her old smile.

'It's funny, but this is like having an erase button. If we both do this, then the things we say now are gone. Neither of us will ever know we said them, let alone what they were.'

Mia frowned. 'That's kind of sad. I guess it's a bit like writing on the sand between two waves . . . It does make me feel braver about what I might say. But also . . . sad. Does it even matter if neither of us remember it?'

'Maybe not.' My finger hovered over the '=' button. 'But I want to say it anyway.'

Mia looked up from her writing. 'Go on then.'

I felt foolish. Even now the words stumbled from a dry mouth, tripping over each other. 'I don't know what love is, Mia. I think that's something I've just started learning about. I know how it starts, though.' We both smiled at that. 'It seems that it grows and changes, and changes you, too. I hope it makes us better. I . . . I'm not saying this very well . . . but I think I'm going to grow into a man who could love the woman you're going to grow into . . .'

193

'That's the most romantic instantly forgettable thing anyone has ever said to me.' Mia signed at the bottom of her page of notes.

'Heh.' I felt my cheeks burning. 'Well, here's me forgetting my half of it.'

I pushed the button.

'You're fine. You're OK, Nick. Just sit still.'

'Mia?'

'Yes. It's Mia. You remember me, right?'

'I remember you.' I blinked to clear the blurring from my eyes. My head ached, a ringing sound faded from my ears, and my mouth tasted strangely sweet. 'We're in the park? I . . . Weren't we at your place? Your mother . . . God! She cut Rust with that bottle!'

'Calm down and read this.' She pushed a notebook into my hands.

I opened it with cold fingers. Pages of my own handwriting. And at the very top, between two asterisks:

kiss the girl

ACKNOWLEDGMENTS

I'm enormously grateful to Agnes Meszaros, without whose beta reading Nick's story would have been very different and far less fun to write. She worked tirelessly and refused to let me get away with anything but my best effort.

I should also thank my editor, Jack Butler, for acquiring the trilogy and for his subsequent support, along with the other editorial staff at 47North. And of course my agent, Ian Drury, and the team at Sheil Land.

ABOUT THE AUTHOR

Photo © 2010 Nick Williams

Before becoming an author, Mark Lawrence was a research scientist for twenty years, working on artificial intelligence. He is a dual national, with both British and American citizenship, and has held secret-level clearance with both governments. At one point, he was qualified to say, 'This isn't rocket science – oh wait, it actually is.'

He is the author of the Broken Empire trilogy (*Prince of Thorns*, *King of Thorns* and *Emperor of Thorns*), the Red Queen's War trilogy (*Prince of Fools*, *The Liar's Key* and *The Wheel of Osheim*) and the Book of the Ancestor series (*Red Sister*, *Grey Sister* and *Holy Sister*).